THE
RECRUIT

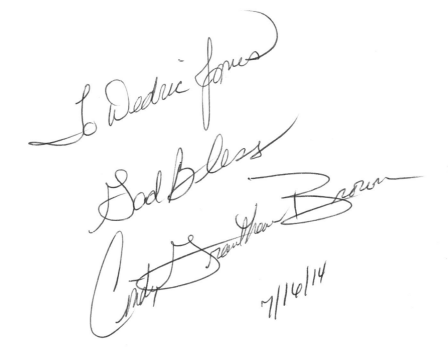

To Dedric Jones

God Bless

Cindy Grantham Brown

7/16/14

THE RECRUIT

Based on a true story

CINDY GRANTHAM
BROWN

Second Edition

TATE PUBLISHING
AND **ENTERPRISES**, LLC

Published by Tate Publishing & Enterprises, LLC
127 E. Trade Center Terrace | Mustang, Oklahoma 73064 USA
1.888.361.9473 | www.tatepublishing.com

Tate Publishing is committed to excellence in the publishing industry. The company reflects the philosophy established by the founders, based on Psalm 68:11,
"The Lord gave the word and great was the company of those who published it."

Book design copyright © 2014 by Tate Publishing, LLC. All rights reserved.
Cover design by Gian philipp Rufin
Interior design by Mary Jean Archival

Published in the United States of America

ISBN: 978-1-63122-609-0
1. Fiction / Thrillers / Suspense
2. Fiction / General
14.04.16

DEDICATION

It is with the greatest appreciation that I thank my wonderful husband, Jackie, for supporting me one hundred percent in all the sleepless nights, birthing pangs and joyous times as well, in the publishing of *The Recruit*.

INTRODUCTION

The Recruit will take you on the ride of your life!
Jess Talbot has already seen sorrow in her young life. One bad decision will destroy her dignity—will she also pay with her life?

At the age of twenty-one, she is recovering from the breakup of her marriage. In an effort to get back into the social scene she hangs out in a park at Memphis, Tennessee along with other rebellious teens and young adults. Here she meets her newest friend, Lisa Burns, who likes to party and hang out with bad-boy bikers. Vulnerable and naïve, Jess goes with Lisa to a Kentucky Motocross Rally for the weekend—which turns out to be anything but the fun, safe weekend she had imagined.

Unknown to Jess, Lisa is an initiate into a biker gang, the worst of its kind. Her job is to find that special girl who will be this year's *recruit*. "To be lifted up before the very throne of God keep a lot of people alive. Would it work for Jess today?" Will Jess figure out what dangers are prepared for her? Will she be forever scarred by her devastating decision to spend the weekend with Lisa and her friends? Will she escape or will the results be deadly for Jess…

Through the grace of God, Cindy Grantham Brown survived the devastating events that this story is based upon. She now tells the fictionalized tale in the hopes that others will never have to face the possibility she did—that of a horrible and painful death, murder at the hands of an evil biker gang.

The innocence of one, the desperation for acceptance of another could cost Jess Talbot her life.

What you are about to read is based on a true story. I have changed the names and some of the locations. Any names I use are not to reflect on any one person or persons. The names I chose are just names not related to any part of the truths. But which is truth and which is fiction? That will be left to the assuming imaginations of you, the readers, to me and those that know the truth.

CHAPTER ONE

It was a beautiful night in Memphis, Tennessee—for some. But out in the back of an old deserted warehouse downtown tension was building as the two small groups were standing face to face waiting on the signal to begin. The odds were against Toby Nelson, the sergeant of arms, and the rest of the members from his club, The Riders. Rex Crest, their elected president, was there along with each member, which brought their total to fifteen. Even being a hundred percent accounted for, they were still outnumbered three to one.

Zack Owen was the president of the Skull & Cross gang. The Skull & Cross were many in number. They had enough members to need two sergeant of arms. This made no difference to Toby, for he was well skilled in martial arts and weaponry.

There was quite a difference in the two gangs. The Riders weren't a gang at all; they were just a group of bikers that really had a passion for motorcycles, Harleys mostly. To fit in or be able to participate in most of the rallies they sometimes had to prove themselves to real biker gangs. Toby Nelson and Phil Moore were fairly new members of just over a year.

It was believed that the Skull & Cross members were connected with a well-known Memphis drug dealer named Denton Vianneh. Vianneh owned most of the nude clubs in Memphis and every attempt to bust him had thus far failed. Oh, he had been picked up several times but somehow was always released. There was never enough evidence to connect him to any crimes. They, the Skull & Cross, were truly a grubby, grungy, dirty group of bikers that were always out to prove that they believed in who they were and what they stood for. Their lifestyle was nothing less than what one might expect or think of in a biker gang. They murdered, robbed, raped, and even worse when they had a notion.

———————

Tonight Toby and Phil would have the opportunity to convince the Skull & Cross that they truly were bikers and prove to themselves that they were as tough as they believed they were.

You could smell the anticipation as the tension gained momentum. The shot was heard and the rumble began. Toby fought long and hard; he first had to defend himself against the two other sergeant of arms, both at the same time. They were well into their fight before the others began.

Toby held his own okay. He dodged more blows from chains and knives than he received. Those he did receive hurt, but not enough to slow him down or defeat him. He took a couple blows to the head, chest, and knees. He even had a trickle of blood running down the corner of his mouth. But those he fought against looked and felt even worse. Toby was much better in martial arts than he had hoped for. It amazed him how much came to remembrance when under pressure, and how his hands and feet just seemed to react instantaneously.

Phil held his own as best he could, but came away with a few more injuries than did Toby. The fight was bloody for all and even deadly for some. Sirens were now blaring and those that could, fled while others were carried out.

The fight lasted about twenty minutes. Too long for Toby's thinking but he survived very well, as a matter of fact, so did the rest of the Riders even though they were outnumbered three to one. The Skull & Cross were whipped ashamedly considering the odds.

By the time the police arrived, there wasn't much for them to see, aside from a few weapons left behind along with blood spills all around. No one was left to talk or be identified.

=—*ৰ৹৹ৰ*—=

One year later...

McKellar Park located on Airways Boulevard in Memphis, Tennessee, was a place of rest, relaxation and recreation. There were tennis courts, an eighteen-hole golf course, pavilions, and a meadow soft with luscious green grass in which to picnic and throw Frisbees, or even take a nap. There were small ponds for fishing, as well as, a convenient rest room area. It even had a hiking and biking trail.

From Airways Blvd at the entrance of the park to the circle drive through and back out to the entrance was only a mile and two-tenths. But on any warm, sunny, summer Sunday during the mid to late seventies, it would take at least two hours to complete the drive through. On Sundays, McKellar Park was more than just a place of rest, relaxation, and recreation; it was a place for drinkers, pot smokers, addicts, and drug dealers to hang out.

You see driving through McKellar Park was the *in thing*.

—⁓—

Jess Talbot was a single twenty-year-old with an uncommonly, but very beautiful, olive complexion and long silky, shiny, black hair. She was a Choctaw, English, Irish, and Welsh mix, your typical American. Although, she was not one to flaunt her assets, she had them. Jess had a quiet and sweet personality. She worked five days, forty hours a week as an inventory clerk for an electronics warehouse on Brooks Road.

It was one of the most beautiful Sundays so far this year. Jess had driven her candy apple blue '71 Mach I, 351 Cobra Jet Special to pick up her newest friend, Lisa Burns. Lisa was seventeen, although she was not much to look at, she was as wild as they came. Jess was sometimes shocked at the language and unusual appearance of Lisa. Most of the time, Lisa wore leather and chains as accessories. Jess had never been around a character like Lisa. Their conversations were intriguing to Jess. She had known Lisa now for a few months and still had not figured her out.

Jess had a drive inside her that wanted to know what made people act or react the way they did. She was often making new friends, just to find out how different people were. But this Lisa character had her puzzled. She knew that there was something different about her; she just couldn't put her finger on it. Not yet anyway. But Jess did not give up so easily on finding out what she wanted to know.

After picking Lisa up around ten in the morning, Jess drove straight to McKellar Park. After about twenty minutes or so into the park, just past the tennis courts, she found an available space to back her car into. It was a known courtesy that when you turned your signal on before an available parking spot, the vehicle behind you would wait to give you enough space to back into it. This unspoken rule was almost always honored.

"Hey look at that green Fiat." Jess squealed with excitement. As the Fiat neared she could see that it was that guy she had been seeing pass through the park for the past two Sundays. "Lisa, it's the guy I told you about. And he's not driving a motorcycle this time. I like his car, which makes me want to meet him that much more." She sighed.

This guy just happened to be Toby Nelson. Lisa knew right off that it was Toby, but she did not want to tell Jess just yet what she knew about Toby. Lisa figured that if she told her that he belonged to a biker's club, then Jess would be turned off and that might discourage her even more about going camping in Kentucky. Lisa was hoping that Toby would be going with his club. *Oh, that would be another possible way to get Jess to go camping. If she takes an interest in Toby and then finds out that he is going... Yep, that just might work.* Lisa had been trying to persuade Jess for several weeks now to go. "If he's not riding a bike, I'm not interested, but I'm sure before the summer's out, you will have him eating right out of your pocket."

"Now, why do you think that?"

"I haven't seen one escape you yet." Lisa said as she lit a cigarette.

"Hey, I don't put them in prison or anything like that." She was fanning her hand in the air trying to ward off the cigarette smoke.

"This is true; after two weeks, you're out looking for someone else."

"I know, but it's just that when they start getting too serious for me or putting too much pressure on me to sleep with them…Well, it's just…it's just time to let them go, that's all."

"That's where we're different, Jess. I like to know the man I'm dating a little better."

"Lisa! You're only seventeen. Slow down a little, you're still in school. You have plenty of time before you should marry." Jess was going into her sisterly mode now.

"Yeah, and look what happened to you," Lisa blew smoke in Jess' direction. She fanned herself again; even with the windows down, there still was not enough clean air for Jess to breathe as long as Lisa was smoking.

"What do you mean by that?" Jess was being a bit perturbed by the question and the smoke.

"I mean you saved yourself for Mr. Right to come along and when he did, you married him. You remember the one that was your first?" Lisa was starting to really get to Jess.

"Yeah, yeah. You don't have to remind me." Jess complained.

Lisa continued. "I know, but let me finish. I want to make a point."

Jess shook her head in agreement with Lisa. "Okay. Okay, go ahead. I'll try to sit through this."

"Oh well, thanks. I mean, don't do me any favors."

"Lisa, go ahead. Seriously, I'm sorry. I'm listening."

"Okay, Jess." Lisa was finding it a little hard to bring up the old past of Jess Talbot. Not that it meant anything to her. She was just trying to make a point, but to Jess it was just reminding her of her very brief marriage to Brad. "It's just, well, what I am trying to say is this... You thought you were doing such a great thing by saving yourself for your husband. That he would be so proud of you for doing that, that it would make your and his relationship more special..."

"It did, at first." Jess said sarcastically.

"*Right*, at first he seemed to respect you for your great service. But you told me that six months after you were married, he forced you to sleep with another man, and he went right into the next room and slept with another woman." Lisa just about had Jess in tears by now. But she didn't stop there. "I don't know why you didn't have the crap beat out of him, leave him, or even better..."

"What?" Jess asked not really listening to Lisa's remarks anymore, they hurt too much. Nor did she want an answer to her rhetorical question.

"Have him castrated."

"I did eventually," Jess answered while her mind was still somewhere else. She was painfully reliving in her mind what actually did take place that horrible night. It was something that she knew would take her a long time to put behind her.

"Have him castrated?"

"Huh? Oh, no silly, leave him. Anyway, get off my case, Lisa. Besides, even though he did me that way, I am still glad I waited."

"My point is that I personally feel that it don't matter if you save yourself for anybody or not. So, I decided I want to be experienced when I get married."

"Lisa, I think you are well on your way."

"You're no saint either, you know, Jess."

"No, but I am very careful about my relationships."

Lisa finally decided to change the subject. "Jess, let's go get some beer."

"No, this is Sunday. And besides, you're a minor."

"It's never bothered you before."

"Hey Lisa, did we come here to argue or to have some fun and check out all the muscles around here?"

"I came to have fun; you're the one who's acting weird. What's the matter with you?" Lisa asked.

"PMS. Sorry for snapping."

"PMS? Wow, that's great!"

"What? Since when did being on your period become so great?"

"Oh, I uh, I mean that you, uh... ummm... have reasons for being so grumpy. Yep that's it." Thinking out loud almost ruined Lisa's plot for the camping trip. If Jess was PMSing this would be an extra bonus for her; but... not for Jess.

Jess couldn't figure her out and was tired of being in that stuffed up car. Even though Lisa had put out her cigarette, the odor and smoke still lingered. "Let's get out." The two girls spread a quilt on the hood of the car. They then settled themselves on top, being sure not to block each other's view.

CHAPTER TWO

"Man, it's a beautiful day. Isn't it, Lisa?"

"Man, yeah. You said it." Just about then a red panel van was heading in their direction. "All right! There's Mickey, my cousin," said Lisa.

"Who? I don't remember seeing that van pull through here before," exclaimed Jess.

"It's my cousin's, Mickey."

"Is he from out of town?"

"Nope, he lives here in Whitehaven."

"How come I've never met him before?"

Lisa seemed to be ignoring her. She jumped off the hood of the car and rushed over to her cousin's van, yelling back at Jess, "I'll be back in a while. I'm going to ride the circle with Mickey. Catch 'ya later."

Jess was about to protest about her not being able to go meet this cousin, until she got a better look at him. He had a full scraggly messy beard and long, unkempt hair. He probably weighed nearly 300 lbs. She shuddered at the thought of even having a conversation with him.

Then...there he was...that cute guy in the little green Fiat. He had made the circle. He nodded slightly, flashed his pearly whites and passed her right by.

Jess, finding it hard to keep her composure, got down off of her car, tossed the quilt in the back seat and began walking toward the tennis courts. She watched as he pulled into the parking lot with ease, stopped, and got out. She tried not to seem interested in any one thing or person, waving at many friends that went by, stopping from time to time to speak to someone in a passing car as it crept along, listening to all the whoops and hollers as guys went by, pretending to ignore them.

——◦◦◦——

"Hey, Mickey."

"Hey, chick, what's happnin'?"

"Not much just checking out the dudes with Jess."

They were riding with the windows down. That was the only way to ride through McKellar Park. The inside walls of Mickey's van and ceiling were covered with red carpet. With all that carpet, it sure was hot in there in the summer time, but it also concealed the noises.

"So, that's Jess."

"Yep, that's her. Did I do good?"

"She looks great, even better than the last one. Have you asked her yet?"

"Sorta. I've mentioned it a few times."

"Well, what are you waitin for?" Mickey was asking in a gruffed-up voice, "We're leaving Friday night."

"Look, I know what I'm doing; I've been working on this one for months now. And I don't intend to lose her."

"Like last time." Mickey said smirking.

"That's not funny." Lisa was getting ruffled now.

"Yeah, I just hope you don't blow it again. Not for your sake only but for mine too. I'm sticking my neck out for you this time. It took a lot to convince Zack to give you another chance so soon, little girl. You know what'll happen to ya if she gets away."

"I'm cool, man, I'm cool. Besides, screw Zack Owen."

"You did."

"Hasn't everybody?"

"Yeah, well, if you mess up this time, you'll not only answer to me, but you know what Zack said he'd do to ya."

"Yeah, yeah! Got a joint?"

"Sure chick. Get the stuff out of the glove box," he said as he was pulling a bag of weed from inside his pants. "Here roll us one."

"Sure thing, man. Got any beer, too?" Lisa asked.

"Yeah, moocher. Help yourself."

After Lisa climbed to the rear of the van to get them both a beer, she settled herself down on the floor behind the seats to roll up a joint. She very carefully sprinkled some Columbian into a paper and rolled it up. When she had finished licking it to stick, she rolled up what was left of the lid and handed it back to Mickey. He deposited it back in to the front of his jeans.

"I want to meet her today." Mickey said.

"I don't think that's a good idea." She said as she was moving up to the front seat.

"Why not? We don't have to tell her anything."

"No, just wait. Let me do this my way."

"Just what is your way?"

"Don't worry man. I'm cool. I'll handle her."

They continued toking away while listening to some Aerosmith. They were just now entering the circle. The park was as full as usual on a gorgeous day like today.

———∽∾∿∾∿∾———

Back at Southaven Christian Church, on the fourth pew sat Jean, Jess' mother, with her best friend and prayer partner, Mae.

Brother Carson, the senior pastor, was at the pulpit that morning. The singing was very uplifting and encouraging, setting the mood for the Holy Spirit as usual.

"'What Are You Speaking?' is my message this morning. In all honesty, it will probably take more than one service to speak to you about what God has been showing me. So be sure and come back tonight to hear more on this subject, providing this subject is the way the Holy Spirit leads. Turn in your bibles to Mark, Chapter 11, verses 20 through 26."

You could hear the pages turning in the almost packed out auditorium of about five hundred as the congregation waited enthusiastically.

Brother Carson began, "Verse 20. And in the morning, as they passed by, they saw the fig tree dried up from the roots. And Peter calling the remembrance said unto him, Master, behold, the fig tree which thou cursed is withered away. And Jesus answering said unto them. Have faith in God. For..."

Brother Carson continued to speak all that had been laid upon his heart. After he completed the reading and at the end of the service, several people came to the altar to make new commitments in their lives and to pray for their needs and the needs of their loved ones. Jean sat at the altar, believing in prayer with Mae that Jess and each of their children would soon be walking with the Lord Jesus and kept safe in this world.

—◦◦◦—

"Hey, Jess." Someone yelled from a passing car.

She smiled and said hello back, not sure to whom she was speaking. Her mind was on the green Fiat ahead of her. She was studying the small sets of crowds standing around in different groups. She would soon be walking right in front of the green Fiat parked in the lot next to the tennis courts.

Where is he? She was thinking out loud as she was now getting closer. There were people all around her that she knew and didn't know. Suddenly, she spotted him. There he was.

The past two Sundays this guy had been dressed in jeans, a black T-shirt, and a leather vest of some sort. Even though Lisa liked the biker look, Jess did not. On more than one occasion he had ridden to McKellar Park on a Honda CC. Not today. Today, he was in a green Fiat and wearing a muscle shirt and blue jeans. He was walking away from his car and her. *Who is he? What is his name?* She wondered. Jess then made a vow that before the day was over she would do her best to find out who he was. There was another guy with him, the same one that was with him the last two Sundays. They were also with a pretty redheaded woman; this bothered Jess.

—◦◦◦—

Oh! Wow, there's Jenni. He's heading right near her. NOW's my chance. Jess walked on over past this hunk to where

Jenni was leaning on the hood of her newly restored red '67 Fast Back Mustang given to her by her parents who gave her everything she wanted.

"Jenni. Hi," Jess said. She could feel his eyes on her as she passed by him. He was leaning on a car a couple over from Jenni's. She was hoping that he liked what he saw.

"Hi, Jess."

"What's happnin' Jenni?" Jess asked.

"Not much, same ole, same ole. How about you?"

"Just looking."

"Anyone I know, Jess?"

"I don't know, Jenni. You tell me. You always seem to know just about everyone out here."

Jenni Smith was just about as plain as her last name. She was slightly overweight, most of the time had a loud mouth, and acted a little over friendly at times. But she and Jess were pretty good friends. After all it was in Jenni's best interest to be Jess' friend since most of the time all the guys usually came around whenever Jess was there. It was also in Jess' best interest to be friends with Jenni. Because of Jess' good looks and Jenni's money, well, there was usually a pretty, good crowd.

"Who'd you have in mind?"

"Do you see that good looking guy over there with that redheaded girl?" Jess asked.

Jenni sighed. "*Yeah*! Isn't he gorgeous?"

Jess didn't turn around to look at him. "Yeah, he is. Who is he? Do you know him?"

"Well, sorta."

"Come on, Jenni. Who is he?" Jess asked with much enthusiasm.

"Listen, if you're interested in him, I'll make a deal with you."

"Nah! Forget it. I'm not interested in him…I'm just standing here feeling all giddy-ish like a schoolgirl kid. Are you kidding? What's the deal?"

"I'll tell you what I know, if when you're through with him, you'll put in a few good words for me."

"*If* I ever catch him, and *If* I find out that I don't like him, which at this point, I doubt. But, yes, I would say good things about you and send him your way, if you're still interested in him. Now, tell me what you know, please."

"Okay! His name is Toby, and he's going through a divorce."

"I sure feel for him." Jess said.

"Yeah, but at least you didn't have any kids involved."

"He's got kids?" This will complicate things.

"No."

"Whew, good."

"Not kids, kid—a daughter who lives with her mother."

"What about that redhead there with him now?"

"Now, that's something I don't understand."

"Why? What do you mean?"

"That's the mother, his soon to be ex-wife."

"Maybe it's not to be so soon, then."

"Oh, I'm sure they are probably still getting their divorce. The whole time they've been over there, he hasn't really looked at her. So, Jess, don't give up hope just yet."

"Well, her being here sure doesn't make it easy to meet him. Especially with her hanging all over him like that."

"Jess, I'm sure it's only her trying to get back with him, and not him trying to get back with her."

"Now, what makes you an expert? How do you know so much?"

"That's what makes me so popular, that and my money."

Shocked at Jenni's bluntness, Jess said, "Jenni!"

"It's okay, I'm used to it."

"Well, Miss Rich Popularity, since she's not so bad looking, why the divorce, especially with a kid involved?"

"I hear she had an affair and he can't find it in his heart to forgive her. Boy wouldn't you two be a comforting match for each other."

"I may never know." Jess sighed as she turned her face away from his direction.

CHAPTER THREE

For a moment Jess and Jenni were caught up in their surroundings. They took a look around. The tennis courts were busy as usual. People were lying around in different places in the grass. Some were playing volleyball. There were a few throwing Frisbees. Some were even playing Frisbee with their dogs. That was always a sight everyone enjoyed watching. You could always hear laughter, fun and enjoyment, whistles, whoops and hollers, sometimes even singing, and on occasion an argument or two. But for the most part McKellar Park was a mellow place to hang out.

"Today might be your lucky day."

"Why, Jenni?"

"Look who's leaving."

Jess turned just in time to hear. "Toby, I hope you lose everything you own." The red head stomped off as she left.

"Losing you is worth it." Toby yelled back at her. "And don't come around me again." Jess could see the anger and hurt in his very masculine face. His jaws were flinching and the muscles in his upper arms were flexing; she could see the tension build. Jess wanted to run up and grab him and hold him in her arms. She wanted to take away his pain. *Wait, wait. What am I thinking? I don't even know this guy.* Her mind was telling her one thing and her heart was telling her another.

Just as she was so pitifully looking at him and thinking these thoughts, their eyes met for the first time since she entered the parking lot. Toby saw concern in her eyes. Jess nearly jumped as soon as she realized he saw her watching him. Her face flushed as she quickly dipped her chin.

Toby liked what he saw and wondered how that horrible scenario must have looked to her. "Jess." An excited voice called from a car beyond Toby; it was Lisa.

"Bye, Jenni, catch ya later." She quickly jumped at the opportunity to walk within a few inches of Toby.

Lisa had something so important to tell Jess that she didn't even notice that she was coming up behind Toby and Phil.

Jess timed it just perfect. When she reached Lisa they were standing almost within an arm's reach of Toby.

"Lisa, where did you go? You have been gone for a long time now." She knew. She was just finding something to say.

"Just around the circle with Mickey, girl, you know how long it takes." Lisa was grinning from ear to ear and stoned out of her mind; it was noticed by everyone including Jess. Just then Lisa noticed they were standing right beside Toby and Phil.

"What have you been doing, while I was gone, man? Or let me guess. You've been making new friends."

Lisa brushed right past Jess and began introducing herself to Toby. Jess was trying to stop Lisa from embarrassing herself, but it was too late. Jess dared not turn around to see the look on Toby's face.

Toby and Phil were both looking puzzled as Lisa rattled on.

"I'll bet Jess didn't tell you that she has a friend who's been dying to meet you?" Lisa was directing this question to Toby.

Jess was removing her hands from her face by now. She couldn't stand it; she just had to turn around to see the expression on Lisa's face when she found out that she had not yet met this man and his friend.

"No, she didn't." Toby was playing along. Jess could hear the sexy masculinity of his voice as he turned to look at her with a sparkle in his eyes.

"Lisa." Jess said. "You've really done it now."

"Oh, don't be embarrassed, Jess, or jealous. I am not out here to put a stop to you two getting to know each other. I'm only here to try and help it along." Lisa was still grinning from ear to ear and was so proud of herself. Toby and Phil exchanged another puzzled glance and shrugged.

"Oh, I'm not so sure you have any idea as to how you're helping us to get to know one another. By the way, I'm not jealous or embarrassed. At least not as much as you should be or will be."

"Why should I be embarrassed or jealous?" Lisa asked.

"Maybe not jealous, but you should surely be embarrassed." *Then again, she probably won't be, in her present state of mind.*

Toby was enjoying every minute of this conversation he was now hearing. He had noticed Jess the two previous Sundays as well. He wished to meet her, but knew he needed to stay focused on what he had to do and didn't need some gorgeous chic distracting him right now. He knew that if he wasn't careful, it could cost him or Phil their lives. "Embarrassed? Why should I be embarrassed? What have you told them about me?" Lisa turned to the two men. "Whatever it was, it's not true, and what are your names?" Lisa gave the guys a look, encouraging them to play along as best as she could. Before the guys had time to answer her, she asked, "Jess, aren't you going to introduce us?"

"How can I, Lisa? I haven't even met them yet."

"I can fix that. Let me introduce myself," Toby played along.

"That wouldn't be proper." Phil was saying as he got off of his Harley.

Lisa was coming out of the clouds by now. "Wait a minute. You mean you all haven't…?"

Her face was indeed beginning to increase a little in color as she couldn't even finish her question. She was afraid that she wouldn't know what to say next. Had she blown it?

"No, we haven't met, Lisa." Jess was enjoying this herself by now.

"Oh, my goodness, what have I done?" Lisa was laughing at everything and all she could do now was grin and snicker a lot.

"Nothing more than the usual, whatever you've been smoking must have been some pretty strong stuff." Jess said.

"Well, I think you have uniquely invented a special way for two people to meet," Toby said, staring at Jess the whole time.

"Whoa! Wait a minute," said Phil. "Again, first let me introduce myself. I'm Phil and this is Toby. Now, tell me your names." He was playing along as well.

Lisa felt a little better as she saw a way out of her blunder, even though she didn't know why the guys were playing along with her shenanigans.

"You already know our names. Thanks to my big mouth, but I'll play along. My name is Lisa and this is my friend, Jess." Giggling, Lisa covered her mouth.

"Hello, Jess. I'm glad to meet you. Toby, say hello to Jess-chick."

"Hello, Jess-chick," Toby said with such a smile that Jess felt like she would melt away.

"Hi, and it's just Jess."

"I don't remember seeing you out here before, Jess." Toby was lying but trying to not let her know that he had noticed.

"Hey, Lisa, you wanna cruise on my bike?" Phil asked.

"Anytime, especially on a Harley," she replied.

"Nothing, but!"

"Come on, man, whatcha waitin for?" She grabbed his arm and got on the back. "Woo-hoo hoo, a '76!"

"Yeah, it is," Phil said as they began to ride off. He was hoping this would be the break that he and Toby needed.

"You better watch her," said Jess. "She's a real Tiger."

Jess then answered Toby's question, "I guess the reason you haven't seen me out here is because I haven't seen you out here much." Her voice trailed as she tucked her chin down and ran her fingers nervously through her hair.

"Yeah, well, I've been pre-occupied with my family." Toby was trying to smooth over what Jess must have heard and seen earlier. But he couldn't tell her the truth. Besides, hanging around with Lisa may mean she might be someone that he wouldn't want to be interested in, but he was hoping otherwise. *Oh well, all in a day's work. I may as well enjoy finding out what I need to know.*

"Oh, are you still living at home?" Jess knew very well that the family he was speaking of was a wife and a child. (Or so she thought.) But she didn't want him to know that she already knew so much about his life. After all that was private and she decided to let him tell her, if he chose to.

"No. I…uh…I have another family."

"Oh!"

"We are in the process of getting a divorce."

"Been there," she said.

"Really?"

"Yep."

"So, do you have any kids?"

"No, do you?" She already knew he did.

"Yeah, I do, she is two."

"Oh. What's her name?"

"Heidi." He hated lying, especially to such a gorgeous chick.

She noticed him lose his ever so captivating smile. "I'm sorry. Maybe we should change the subject." Jess was feeling his hurt again. This was making her uncomfortable. She generally made it a point not to get too close to anyone. She felt she had endured enough pain of her own. But there was something about his face that captured her heart. Not to mention his great muscular body. But Jess was not going to let anyone get close to her again, no matter how good looking he was or how great of a smile he had. *Nope, my mind is made up.*

"I'm sorry. I'm not sad because of my divorce. I'm sad for my daughter. We are taking turns right now until the courts decide. But I am sure they will side with the mother, they always do." He studied the expression on her face as he told her these lies. His fictitious marriage and daughter were used to help him out of situations like this, if and when needed.

There was a silence between them.

He continued with more lies. "I'm the one with grounds for divorce but Heidi is a little girl and she probably needs to be with her mother anyway."

"Yeah, maybe." Jess really didn't know what to say. She only knew she wanted to hold this man right now and comfort him. *Ugh, those feelings, they just won't stay away.*

He knew he had to lie in order to protect his cover, but he wanted to somehow let her know that he would not always be tied down to a child without telling her the truth. He knew he needed to stay in cool biker mode while on the job, but somehow it just didn't seem to matter as much with her. Nevertheless, cool biker was what his job called for, and he was good at it.

"So, enough about me, what's your story?"

"Incompatibility." Even though she knew something about his life, she wanted him to know nothing of hers.

He waited to see if Jess would say more, but she didn't. *Boy, she is going to be a tough one to get information from.* "Sounds easy," he challenged her.

"I never said it was easy."

"Please, forgive me. I'm sure no divorce is easy," he flashed his sexy grin and pearly whites.

"No problem. Even though mine was tough it was probably easier than yours. So, when will yours be final?" She wanted to ask when he would be free.

"In about 6 to 8 weeks, legally." He paused. "But I'm a free man now."

Ahhh, there's that smile again. Great, let's dig for a little more info. "Yeah, I could tell, a little earlier I saw you with a red head. Was that her?"

"Oh, that," he said. "I'm sorry anyone had to hear or see that. Yeah, that was her, Renee, the mother of my child, my soon to be ex-wife." Somewhere in Toby's heart he wanted to tell her the truth, that it was all a set up, he wasn't with anyone, how he really did like the way she looked and talked. He wanted to get closer, to touch her skin, and sense her feel.

"Please, forgive me."

"There's nothing to forgive, honestly. But sure any time." He knew asking her out on a date right now would be moving in a little too quickly, but time was running out. "As soon as this mess is over would you like to go out?" He wanted to tell her the truth but for now he had to let her believe he meant the divorce.

She knew this was quick too, but she hadn't had these feelings in a long time. "Yes, I think I might like that. Let me give you my phone number. Do you have a pen and paper?"

"Yeah, sure do. See, it is right there on the dash of my car, right there, that green Fiat. Help yourself." He could have gotten it himself; he just wanted to see her walk.

As she walked over to his car and back, he was checking her out and liked what he saw. Jess was wearing a deep purple halter with tiny little white flowers, hanging loosely over a pair of white hip hugger shorts. This really showed off those great looking tan legs all the way down to her white lace up sandals. The slight breeze was just enough to make her light, loose top caress and accentuate her body. Yep, Jess is really something to look at. He began to let his imagination run wherever it wanted to. Her skin looked so soft and he was sure that she would smell so good to him. He could almost taste her lips. She returned, "Here it is."

"Jess Talbot, nice name for a beautiful lady."

"Thanks, Toby. What's your last name?" "Nelson, Toby Nelson."

Jess was not as brave or bold as Toby was, she didn't have spoken compliments about him. But there were plenty of them going around in her head.

"We're back." Lisa said as she and Phil were walking over, with her beer can in a brown paper bag. Their trip to the little corner store across from the entrance of McKellar had been a quick one. That was the advantage of having a bike, being able to get through traffic easier.

"Did you two get acquainted while we were away?" asked Phil. Everyone laughed.

"Hey, Jess, I need to get home." Lisa said. She, unknowingly to Jess, had a very important meeting with the gang.

"I'll be glad to take you Lisa," said Phil. He really wanted to spend more time with her in hopes of finding out anything on Zack's gang as he could.

"No, that's okay, Phil, I'll take her. It's time I get home myself." Jess said.

"I'll call you." Toby told Jess. "Okay." She smiled and replied.

Toby gently grabbed Jess' arm and let it slip through his hand until her hand lay gently in his, sending warm sensations all through her body. He stepped a little closer to her. "I'm serious. I'll call you."

"I'd like that very much." Jess was feeling like a schoolgirl getting asked out by a boy for the very first time.

Toby stepped even closer. Their bodies were ever so close. The temptation was almost too much. "How much?" he smiled, teasing.

"I am interested," she took a small step back, "but only in being a friend enjoying the company of another friend." Jess made the point that she wanted him to call, but didn't want him to get the wrong impression. *I don't want him to know how much I'm interested. It's all too fast.*

"Okay." Toby stepped back a little while letting her go. "I'll call you and we'll be just friends then."

"That's what I really want." Jess said just before turning to leave.

CHAPTER FOUR

Jess and Lisa were walking toward her Mustang. Toby's eyes never stopped roaming all over her as she moved across the parking lot.

"Phil, have you ever seen anything more outrageously beautiful than Jess?" asked Toby.

"She is a looker. Lisa's not so much though. I might not like this part of the job after all. Why do you always get the good looking ones?"

"Hey. Look who you're asking."

Phil looked at Toby and shrugged his shoulders.

"This is why." Toby was saying this as he was shaking his head up and down.

"You'll never guess what I found out about Lisa. It's good stuff.

"We'll talk about it later." This had Toby worried a little. If what Phil knew about Lisa had anything to do with why they were here then that meant that Jess was probably involved in it as well. Toby wanted to get to know her but not in that way, he didn't want to get too close and then find out she was involved with Zack's gang. Yep we're definitely going to have to have that talk, and soon.

—⟨ω⟩—

Leaving McKellar Park was nothing to be in a hurry about. Jess finally pulled out on the street. She had to go to the right and all the way through the circle, just so she could be in the correct lane to exit the park.

Lisa was afraid that if she didn't get a commitment out of Jess, now that she had met Toby, she might never get one. She knew that she had to work fast and hard on Jess. "Jess, I have something very important to tell you," Lisa said as she finished off her beer.

"What? That you're out of beer?" They both laughed.

"No, it's about Mickey, my cousin."

"Oh? No, no. I'm not going out with him. Not now, not ever." Jess said.

Well, that's out, now I'll have to go another route. Lisa jumped out of the barely rolling car to drop her brown paper bag and empty Coors can into a nearby trash can and have time to think up another plan.

"Lisa, are you crazy?" Jess fumed, "You could have been hurt."

"I might be crazy but, no."

"You might be crazy but, no. What kind of statement is that?"

"You asked me if Mickey wanted to take you out. And I said, no."

"Oh, good, so what's so important?"

"Mickey has a friend that wants to meet you." Lisa knew she would have to approach this carefully.

"Now, how do you suppose that Mickey has a friend that even knows me?"

"He doesn't really, but Mickey and this friend of his are going to that motocross race this next weekend…" Lisa paused to get a good look at Jess' expression before going on. She couldn't read anything yet, so she continued. "And Mickey asked me to find his friend a date." Another pause while searching her face. "And we could go camping as a foursome."

Jess was taking this all in and wondering just what she really had in mind. She felt something was wrong here but she just didn't know what. Lisa had been talking about this camping trip to see a motocross race for a while now. "I'll tell you what. Why don't YOU go with Mickey's friend and then Mickey can find himself a date and you will have your foursome?"

"Jess, please can't you do me this small favor?"

"Why should I? What have you done for me lately?"

"Well…" Lisa thought quickly. "I did you a favor today!"

"You did? And what was that?"

Lisa had hoped that her blunder of today hadn't messed things up, now she would use it to her advantage. "If it weren't for me and my big mouth, you and Toby may never have met today."

"That is true. I do owe you for that one."

"So, you'll go?"

"Not so fast. I said I owe YOU one, not Mickey's friend."

"But, I owe Mickey a favor and I said I would help. So, I figure if you do this for me and I do this for him, then we will be killing two birds with one stone. Jess, I promise I will never ask another favor of you again." Lisa knew that if she could ever get Jess to go with her then she wouldn't have to worry about asking her for any more favors. She knew that Jess may never speak to her again after this, but she didn't care because her mission would be accomplished. And that's all she was interested in.

"Yeah, right! Just what is a motocross race anyway?"

"Like I've been telling you, it's just where a bunch of dirt bikes race over hills and through mud and stuff." Even though this is what took place, she was hoping that Jess was ignorant to it all.

And being as naïve about Lisa as she was, this put her in much danger. "Sounds so exciting." Jess went on to say with sarcasm. "I'll bet that will be the thrill of my life."

"Oh, you'll never forget it. You have no idea what one of these can do for a person. But you'll never know if you don't go. Come on Jess, I need this favor. Besides it will be a fabulous weekend full of fun, fun, fun. Come on, I'm not asking you to sleep with this guy. Just go with us," Lisa pushed aside the thoughts of what will really happen if she convinces Jess to go.

"Where did you say this was? Hey look, wait a minute; we're fixing to pass where Toby and Phil are. We can get one more look before we leave the park."

Jess and Lisa broke away from their conversation long enough to steal a look in their mirrors to make sure their hair was in place.

"Oh! Oh! Look, here he comes." Jess was trying not to let Toby see her lips move as she spoke.

Toby darted in between cars until he finally came to Jess' car. "Nice car, Jess."

"Thanks. Just a little something I acquired in the divorce."

"I just wanted to apologize for coming on a little strong earlier. I really am interested in taking you out—and just being friends is okay with me."

"That's good to hear, Toby. I really would like to go out with you sometime, and soon."

"Okay, then. I'll see you later. I mean I'll call later. Bye."

"Bye," she was saying as Toby started back across the street.

"I wonder where Phil is. I don't see him anywhere." Lisa was looking over the steering wheel, in the direction Toby had gone.

Jess was finally tuning into what Lisa was saying. "I don't know...wait, look! There he is, over there." She pointed in the other direction, east of the parking lot and across from the tennis courts. "He's over there throwing a Frisbee with those girls. Sorry, Lisa, looks like you'll have to find someone else."

"Yeah, I'm really heartbroken. Man, he's got a nice Harley."

"I think you're more crazy over a Harley than you are a guy sometimes. You talk about them too much."

"Love those Harleys." Lisa said. "It sure looks like you'll be riding in a little green Fiat soon, maybe even watching the sunrise while you're sitting there with the top-down. I can see it now."

"Yeah," Jess sighed. "Only, watching the sunset, not rise."

"Of course you'll be able to thank little ole' me. This brings me back to our conversation earlier. Will you go with me, or not, to the motocross race?"

"Where did you say they were to be held?"

"Bowling Green, Kentucky."

"That's crazy. Why on earth would you want to drive all the way up there just to see some dirt bikes race?" asked Jess.

"We will camp out, and they have a big carnival there every year. It really is a lot of fun. Besides, you hardly ever go anywhere different anyway. You need to get out and do something different. You've been through so much and this will take your mind off of everything, Jess."

"Camping with two strange guys isn't my idea of fun, Lisa. Besides how would you manage getting away for the weekend like that? What will you tell your dad?"

"I'll think of something. He thinks I do no wrong." She was lying but she didn't want Jess worrying about her problems with her dad.

"I thought you wouldn't want to be with two strange guys so I told Mickey that if you didn't want to be with either of them…

"Which, I don't."

"Then we could just go to be going and no strings attached. I also told Mickey that you and I would share the same tent, while they slept somewhere else." Lisa was thinking as quickly as she could to convince Jess to go.

"Well, you just think of everything, don't you?"

"Yeah, and just in case you change your mind, Mickey said all the girls think his friend is good looking."

"I don't care about that; I wouldn't be going for him anyway. It would only be to do you a favor."

"Great then, you'll go?" She was not going to take, "No" for an answer. If she failed she wasn't sure if she'd live through what would happen to her this time.

"I don't know yet. It depends on whether or not Toby calls me."

Lisa was still hoping that Toby was going. She had asked Phil, but he said no definite plans had been made yet. If Toby wasn't going then she would need to think up something evil on Toby to try and discourage Jess from going out with him this next weekend. She would think of something soon, but just in case she needed to lay some groundwork. "I thought you didn't want him to call until after his divorce?"

"I don't, but who knows? I may change my mind before next weekend gets here."

"I don't know, but you probably made it pretty clear to him that you didn't want him to call until after the divorce is final." If Lisa could put a hex on Jess right now, she would.

"Yeah, and it really will be better for both of us if he does wait. But that doesn't mean that he won't and it doesn't mean that I won't."

By now Jess was pulling out onto Airways Blvd. and heading south, then east onto Holmes Road toward Lisa's house. Lisa's parents were very well off financially. They lived in a nice upscale two-story house. She had one brother to share the whole upstairs with. Needless to say, she was a spoiled rich kid.

Unlike Jess, who at the moment was living in a very small one bedroom apartment with her dog, Topper. "Can't we talk about this later? I need to get to Southaven to pick up Topper." Jess always took Topper to her mom's house on Sunday mornings, so he could run and play in the fenced in backyard and be safe while she was out riding around in the park. On occasion, she would take him to the park with her, but not today.

Jess' younger sister, Kara, and younger brother, Bryant, were still living at home with her mom and step-dad, Harvey, and loved taking care of Topper for her. Her older sister, Pamela, and brother, Drake, lived nearby with their kids.

They pulled into Lisa's driveway.

"Do you want to come in for a while?" Lisa was hoping to get her in and get her stoned into making a commitment. Even though Lisa smoked every day she could, Jess rarely drank or smoked anything.

"No, I told you I need to pick up Topper and then I need to get home and get things ready for work tomorrow. But thanks anyway."

"Give this camping trip some thought, okay?"

"Okay, but I'm not promising anything. Bye, Lisa." And with that Jess began pulling out of the driveway.

"Bye, I'll call you tomorrow night and every night this week until you say, 'Yes', to this weekend. I'll not take 'No' for an answer," Lisa said.

Jess waved bye as she was leaving. She knew that Lisa was not going to give up on her. Lisa was very persistent. Jess' thoughts returned to Toby. She just couldn't seem to get him out of her mind.

CHAPTER FIVE

J ess arrived at her mother's house in Southaven. She
rushed in to tell Kara about meeting Toby. "Hi, Mama, I
love you." Jess said as she was passing through the kitchen
and paused to hug her mama. "How was the service?"

"Oh, Jess, you should have been there. It was so good
and many gave their hearts to Jesus today. Several people
asked about you and wanted to know when you would be
coming back."

"That's nice, maybe next Sunday." She said this every
Sunday, and as always, wished she hadn't brought it up, but
only did so because she believed it made her mama happy.
Jess grew up in that church and rarely missed a service;
until she married and fell out of going altogether. She
was once walking close with the Lord but now couldn't
even remember the last time she prayed, really prayed.

"It's about time you started acting cheerful again, glad
to see you smiling." Jean had been quite worried about
her since the divorce.

"Where's Kara? I want to talk to her."

"In her room, resting before tonight's service."

"Hmmm! Smells good Mama."

"Chicken and dumplings, your favorite."

"Thanks, Mama. That will make my day complete." She headed for the den doorway.

"Okay, who is he?"

Jess stopped and turned around. "Who, Mama? What do you mean?"

"There has to be a new man in your life. You haven't acted this alive in a while."

"Well, Lisa and I…"

"Jess, you know I don't like to pry… I know you're a grown young woman now, but I don't like that girl, Lisa. I don't trust her. I think she's trouble." Jean couldn't hold her tongue when it came to this Lisa girl. There was just something about her that Jean didn't like.

"Oh, Mama! You're always so overly protective. Don't worry. Like you said, I'm a grown woman now and I can take care of myself. Besides don't you think all those good godly morals you've taught me are still in my heart?"

"I pray so, dear, I pray so." Just as Jean was about to explain, once again, her reasons for not liking Lisa, she was interrupted.

"Good, because Lisa has asked me to go camping with her and her cousin this next weekend."

Jean didn't like this idea at all. "Are you going? I mean, you just said earlier that you might go to church with me next Sunday."

"That's right, I did…Mama, there'll be plenty of Sundays to go to church with you and a camping trip like this is held only once a year." Jess was now leaning more towards going camping so she would have another excuse to not go back to church. "Besides, you're always telling me I need to see more people and get out more."

"That's right, I do tell you that." In hopes of discouraging her from going camping next weekend, she knew she needed more time than a conversation over dinner. "Why don't you and Topper just spend the night here? Your room is always ready for you. And since Kara is out for summer break, I know she would enjoy spending more time with you tonight."

"Well, okay, but I don't feel like going to church tonight, if you don't mind. Even though you truly are always telling me I need to see more people and get out more often, I don't want to go tonight."

"But camping?" asked Jean.

"It would be a new experience and adventure."

"I can just about guarantee that if you do it with that girl, it will be an adventure, maybe not what you would expect though." Little did Jean know just how right she was. If either of them knew what Lisa had in store for Jess, they wouldn't even be having this conversation right now.

"Oh, Mama." They both knew that Jess would do as she pleased anyway. But they also both knew that Jean was the mother and Jess the daughter and that she would always be treated as such. "Don't worry too much about it, I haven't decided just yet. You see…I've met a guy. Not just any guy, he's a guy I've had my eye on for a while now. And anyway, well, if he calls, I may go out with him instead."

"And just who is this man of your dreams?"

"His name is Toby Nelson. And, you might as well know now, he's going through a divorce and he has a daughter named Heidi. I haven't met her though. Toby seems to think the mother will get custody of the child." She really didn't want her mother to know, but then thought it best that she hear it from her first, should something develop.

"Jess, I think that's wonderful. And I wouldn't judge a man just because he's going through a divorce or that he has a child."

"Good, Mama. Now, I'm going to let Topper in and go talk to Kara."

"Who's child?" Kara asked, as she came into the kitchen. "Hmmm! Smells good, Mama. Chicken and dumplings?"

"Yes, Kara, and Toby's child." Jean said.

"Who's Toby?" Kara asked.

"Why don't you two go somewhere else and let Jess tell you all about it. I need to finish dinner, so we can eat before heading back to church."

"Come on Jess we can go to my room where it's private. Besides, you may want to tell me something about this Toby character that you haven't told Mama, yet."

"Nothing you'd be interested in, Mama." Jess assured her mother as she was being dragged off by Kara. Her mother was praying silently even at that moment for her middle daughter's safety, in case she did decide to go off for the weekend with that Lisa Burns girl.

While Jess was being smothered in kisses by Topper she started at the beginning and left nothing out when talking to Kara. It felt good to share and she knew that Kara was a romantic fanatic and would press her for every detail anyway.

Jess had not felt well the night before and missed that talk with her mom. Of all nights, she could have been dreaming of Toby but the cramping in her stomach would not let her. She lay in bed doubled over in pain. Her mother came in to tell her she was going to be late for work if she didn't get up.

"Mama, would you call Lynn at home and tell her how bad I feel right now? Tell her that as soon as the pain lets up, I'll be in to work, probably after lunch."

"Sure, be right back."

As Jess lay there waiting for her mother to return, Kara came in. "What's all the talk about?" she asked in a sleepy voice.

"Nothing, Kara, go back to bed. It's just those darn ole cramps again. I'll be all right in a little while."

"Jess, I don't know why you don't go to the doctor for that, I'm sure it's not normal to hurt the way you do every month." Kara's voice was trailing off as she headed back to her room to bed.

"Oh, God, please help me to stop hurting so bad."

Just then her mother came in with some medicine. "Lynn said to take as much time as you need. Tomorrow is the beginning of new inventory and she wants you well by then."

"Ugh! I know, that's all I need this week with me feeling so yucky. Why does God let women hurt so much?"

"Dear God said that was the punishment for Eve's sin."

"Eve, where are you now? You need to feel this pain."

"Honey, I'm sure her pains were more than either of us ever could bear. Here take this and thank God for medicine."

"Thanks, Mama."

Jess lay there for a while wondering about God, Eve, and Adam. She then began wondering about her relationship with the Lord. Her mother was a fine Christian woman and had done her best to raise her children to believe in God. *Do I even know God?* She fell back to sleep on that thought.

CHAPTER SIX

"Daniels, Grisham, get in here." Chief Green was yelling. Chief Green was not happy unless he was yelling. Everyone at the Midtown Precinct knew this. Chad Daniels, alias Toby Nelson and Kyle Grisham, alias Phil Moore, were used to their boss yelling at everyone.

"Yes sir, Chief?" They both asked as they walked into his office. The whole front and one side was all glass, even the door was made of a sturdy double pain glass, wire meshed all through. The Chief had insisted on an all glass door hoping to deter people from slamming it. That was something he detested more than anything else. He didn't mind anyone yelling, if they were upset (he did enough of that himself), but *do not* slam his door.

"Tell me what leads you have on the Owen Case." Green was saying as he motioned for Chad to shut the door.

"Chief, we're still working on it." Chad was saying as he shut the door.

Nothing separated the outside commotions from within the office except those sound proof double pained glass windows. Green had made sure that sound proof glass had been installed. His office was not kept very clean from paper work. Green had a secretary but complained he couldn't find anything if she filed it. He preferred to have things lying around the office and in boxes nearby. Pictures of him from his years on the police force hung crookedly on his back walls. His filing cabinets contained papers, but there were probably more on his desk and in his chairs.

"All right, just tell me what you do know about it," Chief Green commanded.

Chad began, "Sir, as you know, we've established our biker identities through the help of Rex and his wife Shelly."

"I know all that, I know that Rex is a former gang member himself. Let's get to what you've found out recently."

"Sir, just as you predicted, working at the Tirestone Plant is going to pay. I did make contact with that Skull & Cross member, Shane Styles. Styles talks a lot and says that he has been screwed a few times by Owen and he's ready to pay him back. Sir, with all that we have on Styles, I think he'll work with us."

"Keep up the good work. I know that you have been working hard on this case. I told you if you'd not rush it everything would work out. Just remember to be careful and report everything *in writing* to me personally."

"Yes sir," they both said.

"Say Chief, I'm really getting to feel like a biker sometimes. After all we've been playing this role for over a year now." Kyle was explaining.

"Sometimes, I take my car," Chad said. He wanted the Chief to hear about it from him first to cover his rear.

"Daniels, it might be cool sometimes but try to ride the bike more than not."

"Yes, sir." No one, not even these two, wanted the Chief on their butts. They knew that getting on his bad side could be their quickest way to being put on foot patrol or pushing papers somewhere in an office. And neither of them wanted that at all.

"Now, tell me, what new information you have on this biker's convention."

"Well, Chief..." Chad started, "nothing really. Everything we know, you already have a report...a written report."

"Have you made any new contacts?"

"Maybe." Kyle said. Kyle received a surprised look from Chad on this remark, but Chad said nothing and just kept his mouth shut and waited anxiously.

Kyle began, and you could tell by the way he was looking at Chad that neither of them had previously communicated about this. "I'm not sure, but there is this chick I saw yesterday at the park," his head alternating from the Chief to Chad. "You know, Chad, the one I took for a ride on my Harley."

Chad sat there in total silence with his ankle resting on one knee, elbows on the arms of the chair, with his chin resting on his doubled up fists, and his eyes fixated on Kyle, while nodding his head in affirmation, slowly.

"Yeah, well, anyway, like I was saying. I found out that she is a fairly new recruiter for the Skull & Cross gang."

Chad sat up more attentive now and wishing that he had been more focused the night before on what Kyle had said, instead of shutting him out, so he could ponder more and more on Jess.

"Now, why do you say this, Kyle?" Green asked "And what does this have to do with this case?"

"Yeah, Kyle, what does this have to do with this case?"

"Well, sir, she went on about how she liked Harleys and was going to own one someday and very soon. Said she had some friends that all had Harley's. We even talked about our gangs, sir she was so messed up. I asked her what her role was in her gang, and she told me that she was a recruiter. I don't know why, but she shut up real quick like."

"That don't mean anything, all gangs have recruiters." Chad cut in sharply. He was hoping that it wasn't true for fear that Jess might be a recruiter as well, and he was hoping for a possible relationship with her. But a *recruiter*? He just couldn't let himself get in a serious relationship with someone like that.

"Simmer down now," the Chief said while gently slapping down at the air with his hands. "Let's hear him out."

Chad tried to not look so anxious to hear what Kyle had to say. He couldn't believe that Kyle was telling the Chief this information before they had discussed it. Kyle had picked up on this, but knew it was too late to stop now. He'd tell what he knew and his thoughts about it and apologize to his friend and partner later.

"Before she clammed up, she said she was working on a chick for this weekend's biker's convention. So, I know they are all still planning to go. That's all. It just confirms that they will definitely be going."

"You, bone head. You're a bone head," Chad said.

The Chief gave Chad a puzzled look, "Good work, Grisham. Keep digging and keep clean. And document everything."

"Yes sir." They said again.

"You, boys, remember that you can't touch them outside of our jurisdiction. Besides I don't want either of you to bust Zack Owen until I give the say so. I'll take care of Vianneh. And that's an order. You got that?"

"Yes, sir," they said. Both were wondering if, when all this hard effort was over, they would really be able to connect Zack's gang and the drugs to Memphis' biggest nude clubs' owner, Denton Vianneh, and the Mayor. All prior attempts had failed. Not this time, if they were lucky.

"Now, we still have our suspicion that they will be bringing back a shipment of Ice from Kentucky. This is said to be the largest Memphis has yet to see. And remember boys, Mayor Braxton's name is not be spoken outside this office pertaining to this case.

"Understood?"

"Yeah!"

"What?" Chief yelled.

"Yes, sir," Chad said.

"Sir, you'll be sure that Zack doesn't get busted before all this comes down, right?" Chad asked.

"No problem. I'll do my part, just be sure you do yours. We've been on this case too long to screw it up. You are my best two agents for this job, or I would have chosen someone else. Now, get out of here and don't forget to meet with Penny, alias Renee, tonight."

"Gotcha, Chief." Kyle said.

They both left the office and walked in silence, through all the noise of cops and criminals and crammed up mazes of desks and file cabinets, to get to their cubicles. This working all night and then coming to the station before getting any sleep didn't happen but once a week and today was that day. Soon they would be going home to sleep awhile before their briefing with Penny at Louigee's Pizza Parlor on Madison, at one o'clock.

"Chad, did you get that date with Jess?" Kyle asked as he pulled his pneumatic lift chair over to Chad's desk, trying delicately to make amends.

"I found out where she worked and called there this morning, but a lady there said she didn't show up for work today. So, I think I'll call her at home after I get some sleep. What about you? Did you ask Lisa out yet?"

"Nah, not yet, I'll probably call her later."

"Say..." before Chad could finish asking what happened back there.

"Look, I'm sorry about what happened in there. I wasn't thinking at first and then when I got started I had to finish."

"Yeah, well, that's okay. I mean if it's true and it may be, then we need to focus on that."

"You know, I'm really not too keen on this idea of taking Lisa out on a date. But all in a day's work!"

"More like a year's work! We can't slow down now, we're too close."

"Yeah, yeah I know, don't worry I'll do my part. But on the next case I get the best looking chick. Let's get out of here. I'm tired."

"Yeah, me too. Let's go." And with that they left the precinct.

———⟡⟡⟡———

"Jess, Jess," came a tender, sweet familiar voice. "Wake up; it's almost time for lunch. Are you feeling any better?" asked Bryant.

Bryant towered in her doorway. He was turning out to be the tallest of her siblings. Her precious little brother.

"Yeah, a little. What time is it, Bryant?"

"It's 11:45. Are you hungry yet?"

"I think I can eat something now. Maybe it won't feel like a solid cannon ball when it hits my stomach."

"I thank the Lord I'm a man."

"Yeah, right; at twelve, you're not a man, Bryant. Don't rush it. You have plenty of time to grow up."

"Well, old lady, let's go eat. I'm a starving, growing little boy."

"I never said you were little. Your just not gown yet."

Bryant put his arm around his older but smaller sister. "Does the old lady need some help to the table?" he said as they went walking through the den toward the kitchen, laughing.

Talk was light as they all ate their cold cuts for lunch. Mrs. Mitchell thought that Jess needed something light for her delicate condition. Bryant was the only protester. He complained anytime cold cuts were chosen instead of a good hot meal. He and Kara always seemed to find a subject that they could disagree on. They sometimes did this just to aggravate their mother, but most of the time Bryant did this just to aggravate Kara.

As soon as lunch was over, Jess went to get dressed. She had decided to go to work as promised even though she felt as if she could stay in bed all day.

When the phone rang she was in the bathroom putting on what little make-up she wore, which consisted of mascara and a little blush. No more was needed.

"Someone, get the phone please, I'm busy," yelled Mrs. Mitchell. "Jess, it's for you." Kara said.

Jess just knew it was Lynn. After all, she was the only person who knew where she was. "Hello," she said.

"Jess, hi. This is Toby. I hope you don't mind, I asked around yesterday until I found out where you worked."

Jess took a quick mental note to be sure and find out who gave him that bit of information. She had her suspicions that it was probably Jennifer Smith. At any rate she would be sure and call her tonight if she got a chance.

"I looked up the number and called earlier this morning; a lady there gave me your mom's number."

Jess was so stunned at his call that for a minute she was at a loss for words.

"Jess, you there?"

"Yeah, yeah I'm here, sorry. No it's, it's fine to call, what's up?"

"The reason I called is to ask would you have dinner with me tonight."

"I, uh, I didn't expect you to call so soon. I mean, I thought we weren't; well never mind." She didn't want him to back out, after all she had been secretly waiting on his call. But she didn't want him to know that.

"Are you saying that you don't want to go out with me at this time or not at all?" Chad was quick to the point. He had two motives here. One was to get to be with Jess and the other was to find out if she was recruiting for the Skull & Cross gang. Chad didn't know that Jess was clueless that she was running with a member of a notorious biker gang.

"Uh, no, that's not it. I mean, you just threw me off guard for a minute but that, that's okay. Thank you for inviting me, and I'd be happy to have dinner with you." It was all she could do to keep her voice from sounding shrill with excitement. Her heart beat ever so fast. She was almost sure Toby could hear it over the phone.

"That's great. Where would you like to go?"

"I like most anything so I'm sure wherever you choose will be fine with me."

Chad wanted to go to his favorite BBQ place on the square but that would be too close to his precinct. He didn't want to risk being recognized for fear someone may come up to him and call him by his real name. If he could keep up this fake identity for one more week it may all be over. Then he could tell Jess the truth, if she wasn't in jail. If Jess was a part of Zack's gang then he would be glad to lock her up, right along with the rest of those filthy bikers.

Not all bikers were filthy gangs. Chad had learned this while staying with Rex and Shelly. They were two of the cleanest and nicest persons anyone would ever want to meet. Rex belonged to the "Used to be Club" group of people that live all over the world that used to do things that were not socially acceptable but have since bettered their morals. So Rex now despised anyone trying to maintain the filthy, grubby, cruel, hateful, and deadly biker's image.

Chad had barely missed a beat in the conversation. "Have you heard of that new place, East Winds?"

"Sure." *Oh, could it be that he's taking me there?* She breathed her lungs full of anticipated air.

"Is it okay with you if we go there?"

"Yeah, that's fine." She was glad that Toby could not see the huge grin on her face at that moment.

"I'll pick you up at six-thirty, we'll have conversation over dinner and I'll have you home at least by ten thirty. I have to be to work at eleven." Chad hated working his cover job at the Memphis Tirestone Plant with Rex, as Toby Nelson.

"Oh, that's fine it's on a work night anyway so that's a good time to be home." And safe! To be out too long with Toby might be too dangerous. Jess was very excited and nervous. "So, I guess I'll see you at six-thirty."

"Sure, now if you'll just tell me where you live."

"Of course, only, can you pick me up at my mom's place? That way she can keep my dog for me." He agreed and Jess gave him the address.

They said their good-byes and hung up.

CHAPTER SEVEN

"Oh wonderful! Wonderful! Wonderful!" Jess squealed, as she hung up the phone.

Kara was standing nearby, snooping really. "Who was it, Jess?"

"Kara, it was him. It was Toby. He's taking me to East Winds out on Ridge Lake Boulevard. That place is so elaborate. What will I wear?" She asked frantically.

"Oh, Jess, how romantic. And don't you worry about what to wear I'll think of something." Kara was known amongst her sisters to have an elegant taste for clothes.

"Okay thanks, but make sure it is appropriate. It's tonight, will you still have enough time to come up with the right dress?"

"No problem. Don't you worry about a thing. But there is a condition to this."

"Name it."

"That you don't spare any details of your date when I see you again."

"Deal. I have to go to work now. Bye!"

Jess left out the door. She knew that Kara would come up with just the right dress. She could think of nothing else during the drive to work. She arrived at one o'clock precisely. She knew to get there before then would have her sitting out in her car waiting on everyone to get back from lunch. Lynn was unlocking the door as Jess found her a parking spot.

"Hey! You must be feeling better," Lynn said.

"A little, but I knew with new inventory starting tomorrow, I had better come in and do my prep work today. It's all mostly a sit down job anyway, so I think I can handle it for a few hours."

"I'm glad you showed up. I know Mr. Meesler will be glad; he depends on your work. Inventory has to be as near to perfect as possible. And you're the best clerk he's had in this place for inventory in a very long time."

"Gee thanks, that makes me feel a lot better, Lynn. I'm glad Mr. Meesler appreciates my work so much. If you didn't tell me these things I may never know it. Mr. Meesler sure is not the type to do much bragging on an employee. Is he?"

"No, Jess, he's not. Look at me I'm his niece, you'd think he would have a few kind words for me, more than he does." Lynn McAfee was the bookkeeper of Lexington Electronics Co., she had been working there ever since she got out of high school. She helped Jess get the job as inventory clerk. Lynn was only a year older than Jess, and she too had a bad marriage. The only thing good that came from hers was Dayne, her son. Jess had a lot of respect for Lynn; she had really strong bible beliefs. Even though it had been awhile since Jess last went to church, she promised Lynn she would visit soon. At least it would be a familiar one. Lynn and Jess' mother were members of the same church.

"Good afternoon, Ladies." Mr. Meesler said with a huge smile on his face.

"You're in a good mood, Mr. Meesler. Are you having a good day?" Jess asked as Lynn went on into her office and shut her door, but not before hearing Mr. Meesler's comment.

"Jess, seeing you here this afternoon has made my day a much better one. If there's anything we need around here, it's employees that will show up for work."

Lexington Electronics employed three others besides Lynn and Jess. There was Martin a stock boy and counter sales clerk, Johnny the sales counter manager and Ed, the salesman.

"Yes, Mr. Meesler." Jess replied. She was looking at Lynn through the big glass window in front of her office as she went on into her small office containing two chairs, a metal shelf stocked with books and a few personal mementos, a couple of pictures of her with Topper, and on the desk a note pad and a telephone. She closed her door and began setting up the paperwork for Tuesday's inventory. With her stomach cramping the way it was, she was sure glad to be sitting down for most of the day.

———✧✧✧———

"Chad, when did Penny say she'd be here?"

"Should be any minute now."

"Well, she needs to come on."

Chad and Kyle sat in a booth at a little midtown pizza parlor operated by Sal Louigee, a retired police officer.

Sal had decided that after retirement from the force, he would run a government-funded restaurant. A place where cops, undercover cops, city officials, and of course the feds could come and eat in peace without having to worry about their cover being blown. The way Louigee's was set up, each booth had a little bit of privacy.

Sal's wife, Doris, came to their booth to take their order for a large supreme pizza with a pitcher of Dr. Pepper, and three glasses, nothing to eat for Chad—soon he would be taking Jess to dinner. Penny came in just as Doris was leaving food and refilling their drinks; she took Penny's order and left. They exchanged their hellos before Penny sat down.

Chad, Penny, and Kyle reviewed each other's notes in hopes they might come up with something they may have missed.

Penny had been brought in on the case a couple of months into it. She knew that she was more of a cover for Chad than anything else.

"Do you think we've convinced anyone interested that we're getting a divorce?"

"Yeah, Penny, You should take up acting, maybe you'd land a job in a movie." Kyle teased.

Chad was thinking, hoping that Jess was one of those interested. Penny did not mind it so much when she heard about the possible lead Chad had with Jess. But when Kyle spoke of what his plans were for him and Lisa, Penny's eyebrows raised, her jealousy became obvious. She was hoping that no one noticed as she sat there next to Kyle. Kyle and Chad exchanged knowing glances. Kyle thought that maybe this would turn out to be the perfect situation after all. He didn't have to hide his true identity from Penny. Maybe something could develop from this.

Kyle and Penny talked on as Chad sat there in silence for a while. He wanted to get home as soon as possible; his thoughts were busy on his dinner date with Jess. He was sure glad that he didn't have to show up at the precinct the next day, which meant that he could go straight home from work and sleep all day; he was sure going to need it.

Kyle and Penny warned Chad to be careful and not fall too quick. No one knew Jess' involvement in the case. Is she a gang member, recruiter, or someone the gang is going to recruit? Chad was thinking and hoping she was innocent. *If she's a recruiter, then it's just a job, and I'll finish it properly. If she's to be recruited, then I have other things to worry about.*

Jess was having a hard time keeping her mind on her work. Inventory required a lot of attention and clear thinking, which was hard to do when all she wanted to think about was what she would wear tonight, and what it was going to be like with Toby. She could almost feel his body touching hers as they danced in her head. *Danced? Can you dance at East Winds?* She didn't know for sure, but she was hoping. If you can dance there, then I can be close to Toby and smell his cologne. Jess was a dreamer. At this rate, she would not be finished by five. She knew she needed to stop dreaming and concentrate.

Five o'clock finally did roll around; Jess tidied her office and headed for the door.

"Jess?" It was Mr. Meesler. "Yes sir?" She asked.

"Would you be willing to work some overtime this week?"

She dared not jeopardize her job, but job or no job did she have guts enough to say what she was thinking? You could almost read this crazed expression on her face. Yes, she did. "Yes sir, Mr. Meesler, I would love to put in some overtime this week." He smiled. Good, so far. She had hoped to soften him a bit before saying, "But not tonight. Is it okay if I start tomorrow?" Jess was holding her breath while trying to look brave and confident.

He began rocking back and forth from his heels to his toes, with his hands held behind his back, scrunching his face and rolling his eyes.

Uh-oh! Here it comes he's going to tell me how much he needs me tonight. And really, he did.

Then all of a sudden he stopped rocking, released his hands, and a big smile came over his face. "All right, I'll see you early in the morning and don't be late."

Jess' mouth began to drop open, but she caught herself. "Thank you, Mr. Meesler. Yes sir, I'll not be late; I'll see you in the morning. Bye now," and out the door she went.

She had to stop by the cleaners to pick up her dress. Actually it was Kara's dress, but she had insisted on Jess wearing it. They both borrowed each other's clothes all the time. When she got to her mom's, her stepfather, Harvey Mitchell, was getting out of his truck. He had just come home from work.

"Jess, Hey! I hear you've got a hot date tonight."

Jess was getting ready for him to say something funny. Harvey always had some cheerful thing to say. Even though he was a recovering alcoholic, he had been a good dad for them. Jess' real dad had remarried and moved to Arkansas. Jess was thinking about all this as they walked into the house together.

"Where's he taking you?"

"East Winds, It's a Chinese place..."

He interrupted her. "I know about that place." He attempted to pull at his eyes and buck out his top teeth. "You'll eat food that you have to suck between your teeth and you'll come out looking like this." He showed her.

They both laughed as they entered the house. "What's so funny?" Her mother asked.

"Jess is going out with a China-mon tonight."

"Oh, Harvey, I am not. He's a wonderful person. You'll see, tonight, when he picks me up." She was telling him as she rushed off to shower and get ready for the date.

Kara was waiting on her when she got out. She had already laid out all the undergarments that would be needed to go with the dress.

"Kara, I don't need to wear a sexy garter belt with stockings like that. Panty hose will do just fine. I am NOT going to let him see beyond my dress."

"Oh! Please wear it? For me anyway. Besides when you wear something like this, it makes you feel more like a woman. And when you feel more like a woman, you act more like a woman. Men like that. It will just make your night more romantic."

Jess started to ask her sister just how she knew so much about what men liked about women and then thought of all those romance novels that Kara reads. They were nice enough novels but nevertheless they were romance novels. "Oh, all right, I'll wear it. I need some romance in my life right now," sighing as she starred displeasingly at herself in the mirror.

"Are you feeling okay, Jess?"

"Yeah, I'm just nervous. Did you plug in the hot rollers?"

"Yes, and the curling iron, and I went out and bought the best kind of hair spray for your hair."

"I wish my hair was as thick as yours."

"If it was, you'd want hair like yours."

"You're probably right. Well, how do I look?"

"Jess, that dress looks better on you than it does on me."

"Oh, you're just saying that to make me feel good, Kara."

Kara led her sister by the shoulders in front of the full length Cheval mirror. "No. Look."

And look she did.

Kara left the room to go check on the hot rollers. Jess stepped back to get a good look at her slim figure. She did feel a little pleased at how she looked. The dress was a smooth floral print of soft pastels with a touch of purple and mauves. The sleeves fell gently between her shoulders and elbows. Its neckline had a sweet heart collar that lay perfectly across her chest just above her cleavage. The body of the dress complimented her shape, clinging all the way to just below her slim thighs. There it flowed into small gathers that softly hung to just below her knees. The material was a sheer fabric that required a full length slip to match. Of course Kara saw to it all.

"Jess, come on in here; it's time to fix your hair," Kara called from the hall bathroom.

At precisely 6:30 p.m. the doorbell rang. Kara had just put the finishing touches to Jess' hair. Jess had applied a little more make-up than usual, which of course made her even more beautiful than ever.

"Every old barn needs a new coat of paint once in a while," she had told Kara. She could hear the introductions being made in the living room.

"I'll go get her." Mrs. Mitchell very politely said.

"Mama, how does she look?" Kara asked.

"Like a picture. And let's hope he treats her like one. Admiring her but not touching her."

"Oh, Mama!" exclaimed Jess.

She entered the room. All eyes were on her. Even Harvey was at a loss for words. This was a rarity.

"Whoa! You look great, Jess." Chad was taken back a bit by her beauty. He took her by the elbow. "It was nice to meet all of you," he said while nodding his head politely and easing her toward the door. Harvey didn't like Toby's reaction.

"Thank you, Toby. Let's go." He opened the door for her. "Bye everyone don't wait up. I'll get my car tonight, and I'll come pick Topper up after work tomorrow."

She walked ahead of Toby to the Fiat. But Toby was quick enough to be there in time to open the car door for her. He had also made a point to have the top up, so the wind would not blow her hair. Kara had done an outstanding job with her flyaway silky hair. Jess' hair hung down below the middle of her back, even with all those curls. Curls that Toby just couldn't help but gently fondle, after he got into the car. He handed her a box of chocolates. "These are for you. I hope you don't mind."

"I don't know of anyone that would mind chocolates, except my dad. He doesn't like chocolate."

"Harvey?"

"No, my real dad. My parents divorced when I was fourteen. My dad remarried and now lives in Arkansas. And thanks for the chocolates."

"Sure. I made reservations for seven. We better go. Even though we may have to wait a couple of minutes after we arrive, we need to be on time." And with that he backed out of the driveway. Driving away, he couldn't see the four pair of eyes peeking out from behind the curtain in the living room. They were all smiling and waving until the Fiat sped around the corner.

CHAPTER EIGHT

"Hey, Chick! What's happnin?"

"Not much. You got some weed?"

"Yeah, but not until you tell me some good news."

"Just what might that be?"

Zack stood and grabbed Lisa by the hair. He was pulling her to her knees. "Don't get smart with me, chick. You haven't earned the right yet."

"Oh, yeah! You just have no idea what this little chick can do." There were tears in her eyes, but there was no way she was going to show any weakness.

"I just might have to find out. But until you get so lucky…did you find a sweet little recruit for this weekend, or not?" He released her.

"Yeah, man, I said I would didn't, I? Zack you know I'll do whatever it takes to earn my right with the Skull & Cross."

"Well, chick, this is initiation time.

They all were cheering, whooping, and laughing at this.

The parking lot at East Winds was full. But Chad found it easy to park his Fiat in small places. He told Jess to wait as he got out of the car. He wanted to be sure to impress her with a gentleman's way of doing things. Besides he wasted no chances of being close to her. He gently helped her out of the car. He placed his very masculine hand ever so slightly around the back part of her tiny waistline as he escorted her into the restaurant.

The hostess greeted them at the entrance way. "Do you have a reservation?" she asked.

"Yes, Nelson is the name."

"Yes, Mr. Nelson, your table will be number nine. It will be ready in about twenty minutes. Would you care to have a drink while you wait? Compliments of the house?" The first drink was always a house complimentary. This was just to get people started into drinking more.

"Yes, of course. That would be fine."

"Right this way, Mr. Nelson."

Chad naturally waited to make sure Jess would be walking in front of him. He was the perfect gentleman. Jess was noticing all the stares and smiles that were being directed at Toby from all of the women in the lounge-room as they entered. Chad also noticed all the stares but kept his cool and looked unbothered. Jess admired him for this control he had about his looks. If Jess had not been with him, though, he may have noticed even more. But he couldn't help but notice the looks and stares that Jess was receiving from all the men in the place.

They were seated at a table. "You're complimentary wine, miss, sir." The waiter set the drinks before them.

"I am Wong. I will be your waiter for the evening. Is there is anything else you would like, maybe an appetizer before dinner?"

"Jess, would you like something while we wait?"

"No, I think this wine is enough for now. Thank you." Jess did not want to tell Toby how her stomach was still cramping and how hard it was probably going to be for her to eat. She wasn't even sure of what to order.

"Did I tell you how beautiful you are?"

"You might have mentioned it."

"I want you to know how beautiful you are to me right now. You have this look about you that makes me very... mmm... proud to be with you."

"Whoa, you really know how to lay it on. Don't you?"

"If the reason is good enough, and with you it is. You are an attractive young lady that turned the head of every man in here tonight. I'm sure you have made their evening a pleasant one, as well as mine."

Jess blushed at this.

Chad had something he was going to ask her but he wanted to be careful. "Jess, the other day at the park, your friend, Lisa, she isn't messed up in a motorcycle gang, Is she?" Chad thought this was the best way to find out if Jess had anything to do with the gang.

Jess was a bit confused at his question. "Why do you ask that?"

"I don't know. Maybe the way she was dressed or something."

Jess remembered that Toby had been dressed similar twice before, that she knew of. What if he is into bikes, gangs, and things? If he was then she knew that she didn't want to have anything to do with him. *What if Lisa is too! If she is, is he interested in her? Well, if they both are, then they can have each other.* "No, I don't think Lisa is part of a gang. She would have told me so."

"Good, then I think that's great news." He could tell by the way Jess answered his question that she did not approve of such things. *Or is she good at covering up the truth? After all, maybe she's as good a liar as I am.*

Now Jess was truly confused. *If he wants Lisa to be part of a gang then why was it great news that she isn't? Or, is he being truthful about his feelings? Oh, how I want to believe the best, but there is something suspicious, I just can't put my finger on it.*

Chad reached across the table to take her hand in his, trying to change the subject now and return to safer ground. Their eyes were taking in all they could of each other. "Jess, let's dance." He was already on his feet lifting her gently by her elbow. He was not going to give her a chance to say no and she was just as pleased to change the subject. They made their way onto the dance floor. The music was perfect. This was their chance to be next to each other.

She laid her head gently on his chest. Mmmm, the smell of his cologne fits him perfect. This dance is perfect. The night is perfect. Maybe he is perfect?

"Jess, thank you for having dinner with me."

"I'm glad you asked."

"I almost didn't." This brought her head up and eyes looking straight into his baby blues, searching. "I mean, I almost waited until after my divorce to call you. But I found out Sunday that Renee is going out of town this weekend. And she will be gone for about three weeks. So, Heidi will be staying with me until her mom gets back. Which is okay, I mean, I love to have her with me. It just means that for two weeks or maybe three. I won't be going anywhere. And I wanted to ask you out before then."

"Oh, well, I'm glad you did. Besides, I may have plans for this weekend. So, that will be a good time for you to spend with your daughter." She said this but just couldn't imagine him having a child yet. But why not, he was definitely old enough. And three weeks… that's a long time to wait.

"So, just what are your plans for this weekend? Not that I'm trying to be nosey, just asking." Chad was indeed being nosey.

"Four of us are going camping." She didn't want to tell him where or with whom.

He smiled at this. If she was going camping with just three other people then she definitely wasn't going with a gang of bikers. He held her a little tighter, without realizing it, but Jess was very aware.

"Table nine, table nine. Table nine is ready for Mr. Nelson and company," was called from Wong, their waiter.

"That's us, Jess." He was leading her off the dance floor.

Jess was so caught up in being in his arms that she never heard the call. "Oh, of course."

After they were seated, a chef prepared their food for them at their table. Each table had its own personal chef. Several couples sat at the same table and watched the chef toss knives through the air and catch them at precisely the right time to let them come down and slice the meat and vegetables as was needed. It was a memorable event in itself.

Chad and Jess enjoyed this performance and each other's company. They talked with the other couples at their table as well. Everyone laughed at the jokes and stories that were being told.

It was around 9:30 p.m. when they left the restaurant. Jess had been able to eat more than she had anticipated.

As soon as Chad had her in the car and was seated himself he leaned over and kissed her on her temple. "Would you like to see where I live?"

"*Noooo*," was softly drug out. "Not tonight." Her head still leaned against the seat, eyes closed. She wanted him to kiss her again and again and again... but "Not tonight." She opened her eyes and lifted her head. They smiled at each other and he started the engine.

The ride home was silent. They stole glances at each other when they could. Thoughts of pleasure were going through their heads while leaving dreamy smiles on their faces.

He pulled into her mother's drive, so she could pick up her car, came around, opened the door and walked her to her car. He again kissed her temple. "Can I call you again?"

"I'd like that, Toby."

"Jess, I had a good time."

"It was just what I needed. A nice dinner, out with a decent guy, and back home at a decent hour." She had hoped for at least a good night kiss.

Chad pulled her body close to his. "Toby," she whispered softly.

"Jess, I just want to hold you for a few minutes more. It may be awhile before I can do this again. After all, there's Heidi this weekend, and you're going somewhere with…?"

"I haven't said I'd go yet. Lisa has some idea of a camping trip with a couple of friends."

"What's the matter? Don't you like camping?" He so wanted to hear her say that she wasn't going to go with Lisa. He was near one hundred percent sure that she didn't have a clue as to what she could be getting herself into. How could he tell her, warn her not to go without blowing his cover? How could he stop her from going? He didn't really know her well enough to just step in and demand her not to go; it probably wouldn't do any good anyway.

"Yeah, I guess so. I'm just not sure if I want to go this weekend." She wanted him to say that she was invited over to meet Heidi this weekend, and then she would have a good reason for not going camping with Lisa and her cousin.

Chad knew she was hinting but he couldn't ask her out for this weekend. This weekend would probably lead to one of the biggest busts in Memphis. And he couldn't tell her why he couldn't ask her out either.

They lingered a while longer before saying their last good-nights.

She watched as Chad drove away. She had not had feelings like this in a long time.

CHAPTER NINE

"Chad, Chief wants to see us in his office. You too, Kyle," Penny was telling them as she walked over to their desks.

"Come in, come in. I've got some news I thought might interest you."

"I haven't told them anything, sir." Penny said.

"What is it, Chief?"

"Daniels, my boy you and Grisham are sitting on a keg of dynamite that is about to explode."

"Sir, what do you mean?" asked Grisham.

"I had Penny, here, go on a date with Styles, which was very enlightening. Tell 'em Penny, what you found out."

"Wait a minute! Uh, sir…if you please, when did this take place?"

"Last night, Grisham," replied Chief Green.

"You mean you weren't really sick, Penny?"

"No, Kyle, I was playing detective."

"But why weren't we told?" Chad asked.

"This was something that came up all of a sudden and just, before Penny was getting ready to leave to relieve you is when I found out. I knew that I couldn't reach you by phone, and I don't want anyone but us four to know about it. So, the message you got was that Penny was sick and couldn't make surveillance."

"Yes, sir. We now understand that, but what is so important that you want to tell us?" asked Chad.

"You must understand the importance of the secrecy of the Owen case." Chief Green went on. "Not one word—I mean not one—is to be leaked out of this office. Do you all have this clear?"

"Yes, sir," they both replied.

"We have found out who the Owen gang is bringing their shipment to on Sunday. Now all we need to know is the location"

This was disturbing news to Chad and Kyle. They had been working on this all week and couldn't get anywhere. But they listened in silence.

"I know what you're thinking. How come I found out before you guys did. It really was due to all the work you three have been doing out in the streets. It seems that we have a snitch somewhere in our department. But I'll handle that one. From now on anything you know or need to report, do it directly to me. Don't even use our inside lines. You may call me at home or see me personally."

"Yes, sir, we understand." Chad said.

The Chief went on, "I got an anonymous phone call yesterday as soon as I got home. The caller said that you two guys were on the right track. He said that Owen was bringing in a shipment of ice Sunday. He said that he would be delivering it to a hot shot lawyer by the name of Jack Rands."

"Rands?" You could hear the disbelief in both their voices.

"Yes, Rands." Penny said. "Can you believe it?"

Neither of them answered her; they both were too stunned to say anything, but the questions they had rolling around in their heads just wouldn't stop. After what seemed an eternity of silence, Chad finally found his tongue. "Chief, are you talking about the same Rands that works at the Colton & Rands Law Firm on Riverside Drive?"

"Rands himself is the one I'm talking about."

"So, do you think it's Rands, on his own, doing this?"

"Grisham, that's what we're going to find out. It's possible that he's not working alone. We have to assume that he is not until we can prove otherwise."

"If he's not, then that means that maybe his client is involved," Chad said.

"He has more than one client, doesn't he? I mean how many of his clients can be involved?" Kyle asked.

"Oh, come on Grisham, think about it, now. Which of his clients that we know for sure owns over half the strip tease joints in Memphis?"

"Vianneh," said Kyle.

"Not to mention that he is also the Mayor's personal attorney," said Penny.

"Yeah, I know, Penny, but that doesn't mean he's the one involved," said Kyle.

"I can't believe what I'm hearing, Kyle. We've been working together for six years now. I know that you know how much we've all wanted to shut him down," said Chad.

"Yeah, Chad you're right, it's got to be them behind all this."

"Glad that's settled. Now after I got that call yesterday, I traced it to Shane Styles. I hurried to catch Penny before she was to go out on surveillance with you, Grisham. I needed her to try and get to Styles somehow."

"Yeah, and did it work!" exclaimed Penny.

"So, Penny really didn't get sick and have to miss surveillance last night. You were working after all." said Daniels.

"I'm the one that had to pull surveillance alone for a while. I should be the one complaining."

"Kyle, I'm not complaining about Penny, I'm just trying to put everything together. Besides, I told you I had to work through Jess to try and find out anything she might know that we don't yet. So, go ahead Chief, tell us everything we need to know."

"Penny was able to run into Styles as he was leaving a liquor store down on Union last night. She was able to convince him to leave with her."

"Yeah, and once he agreed we went to a room that the Chief had rented downtown."

"Yeah, some sleazebag motel on Riverside Drive. I was there waiting on them," Green said.

"You mean you played the part of a hooker?" asked Chad.

"I didn't have to. I just convinced him that we knew that it was him that made that call and if he didn't want any trouble from us, he had better come with me. Once in the room he sang like a bird. He claims that Mayor Braxton, Denton Vianneh, and Jack Rands are working together on this. He said that he is bringing the shipment in to Jack Rands on Sunday. He claims to not know exactly how much is being brought in. He said he's only the go between for Owen and the others. So what if he takes a little cut for himself? It can't be too much or they'd notice and he wouldn't risk getting himself killed by them in case we don't bust them. He did say that he heard enough talk to know that Memphis has never seen a shipment so big. He said he really didn't like Zack Owen or any of his gang. So he would do anything to see them locked up. This Shane Styles is the perfect informant. I don't think we have to worry about him speaking to any of the Skull & Cross gang about our conversations." She continued. "Styles is supposed to leave out with the Skull & Cross bikers Friday night and try to get away early on Sunday morning and come back to Memphis before the others so he can tell us for sure if the shipment is coming in or not."

"Penny, that's if he gets a chance to find out anything about the time and exact location of the shipment." said Chief Green.

"Daniels, which is why I have decided that you will be going to Bowling Green this weekend."

"But, Chief." Chad knew this would interfere with his plans to take Jess out, providing she was not a "Recruiter" with the Skull and Cross and wasn't going to Kentucky.

"No arguments. And you are to ride there with them so you can see to it that Styles makes it there and back. Once you've identified their carrier, time, and exact location, and you'd better, then you are to head back to Memphis, but don't leave before Sunday or you will look suspicious to them. You got all that?"

"That ought to be interesting." Chad said with a look of surprise.

"How is he going to bring it all in? I mean what are his plans?" asked Kyle.

"He has a future buyer lined up to meet with Zack on Sunday." Chief Green was explaining. "And Daniels you are the link to that buyer."

"Whoa, yes sir. But where do we meet?"

"We won't know that for sure until Styles gets back on Sunday." said Green.

"So do you think that either of Rands' clients will be at the drop?" asked Kyle.

"Grisham, I don't even know for sure if they're in on it. Just because Styles says they are doesn't mean they are. I know we've had our suspicions, but they've always slipped away. If they are, let's hope they'll be there. If they aren't then we'll intercept and make a deal with Rands and the others. We'll pull this off yet. We've been working on this too long to blow it or let those three slip through. But, I do know one thing for sure. This is not to leave my office. Remember, there is a leak in the department. I also know that I'll find that leak and bury him."

"A leak," repeated Chad.

"Yeah, so don't call me here about this case, either come see me in person or call me at home. If Vianneh, the infamous night club owner, and our mayor are in on this then this will be the biggest bust in the history of this police force. I might even let it slip out that Sunday there will be no real big arrest made. Maybe then our leaker will get that message to Rands and on to Vianneh and Braxton. Either way, we have Owen, the Seller and all the buyers. Hopefully, if need be, Grisham you'll be the future buyer to connect up with Owen. Styles has them believing that you just want to see if the operation runs smooth before you introduce them to a future buyer."

"But for now just go on being Nelson and Moore doing whatever it is you have already planned. Go on home for now, I may need you in a little while. I'll call you if I need you. Go. Get out of here, but not a word. I'll let you know something as soon as possible, I promise." Green was wrapping up. "Oh, and just one more thing— you're all doing a great job out there. Just be careful not to screw this up. We sure can't afford to screw things up." They all agreed, and went quietly out to the parking lot.

"Penny, where are you going?" asked Kyle.

"To get a bite to eat and then home. You want to go?"

"Yeah. How about you, Chad? You want to go with us?"

"No, not this time. I need to make a phone call."

"You got to eat man. I'll bring you over a hamburger on my way home," said Kyle.

"Okay, thanks…I got to go, man, right now I'm in a big hurry to make that call."

CHAPTER TEN

The rest of the week at the electronics store had Jess running ragged. The only two good things about today for her were that she had finished putting in her inventory by five o'clock and she no longer had to put up with cramping, at least not for another month. It was finally Friday. Lisa had called her every day and was really beginning to be a nuisance. Jess would give Lisa her answer today.

Topper waited patiently for Jess to get out of the shower. Jess no sooner had gotten dressed, when Lisa phoned.

"Hello."

"Jess, hi. Are you ready?"

"No, Lisa, I'm not going."

"Not going? But you must go! Jess, I need this favor."

"I'm just kidding, Lisa. I'll be ready at around seven. Who's picking me up? Or do I need to come to your house?"

"No! Don't come to my house. Mickey and I will pick you up. You'll be at your mom's house, right?"

"Yeah, she is keeping my little Topper for me." She said this while scratching Topper's favorite spot behind his ears. "Say, what's his friend's name, anyway?"

"Dave, but he won't be with us. He lives in north Memphis. Mickey thought it would be much more convenient for us to pick you up first. So, I'll see you around seven then. And thanks Jess. You have no idea what a favor you are doing for me."

"I thought this was a favor for Mickey."

"It is, from me. I'll explain it all to you later. But not until you have told me every little detail about your date with Toby." She hoped that by then Jess wouldn't be able to remember her question about favors. If everything went according to her plan, she wouldn't even know where she was for a while.

"Okay, bye. I'll see you when you get to my mom's."

"Great! Bye."

"Dad, Jess is having trouble with her car. So, I called Mickey to see if he wasn't too busy to give me a ride to her house. He said he didn't mind."

"Lisa, how come she can't use her dad's truck or her mom's car?"

"Jess called and said her dad would be working late tonight. And her mom is doing some last minute shopping for the camping trip."

"You didn't have to call Mickey. I can take you to Southaven. I think it was nice of Jess' parents to invite you on this trip, and it will give me a chance to meet and thank them in person. I'm sorry Mike has to use your car for now. It's just until his gets fixed."

"Dad, thanks for offering to take me. I'll try to reach Mickey before he leaves the house." *What to do now?* She had to think, and quick. Of course Lisa did not even really dial the number, she just pretended. She actually dialed JAM-JAM-1. She listened to the recording of the time and temperature.

"Hey, this is Lisa. Is Mickey there?" The recorded voice continued to repeat the time and temperature. "No, I was just going to try and catch him. Dad said he would drive me to Jess'. That's okay. I'll tell Dad."

Lisa's dad was standing there listening to the conversation which wasn't. Lisa hung up the phone.

"Sorry, Dad, he left already. But that's okay. I'm sure Mickey doesn't mind taking me."

"You're probably right. Thank Jess' parents and Mickey for me. If you get into trouble this weekend and you need your dear ole dad to bail you out, you call me."

"Dad, I'll be fine. I'm sure Jess' parents will take good care of your little girl."

"Maybe I should call them and let them know how much I appreciate their kindness to my little girl."

"No, Dad, please don't. You'll embarrass me. They might think I'm a baby."

"Lisa, you are a baby…"

"Dad, I love you." Lisa gave her dad a hug, and smiling the whole time thinking of how she was outsmarting him.

"Lisa, I'm glad to see you hanging around people like Jess. I knew you would see it my way about those hoodlums you were running with. A young lady, or anyone for that matter, does not need to be around such filthy people as bikers."

"Yeah, Dad. Thanks for helping me to see the truth."

"Anything for my only daughter. I'm off to the club since Mickey is picking you up. You be careful and have a good time. Do you know what time you'll be home Sunday?"

"No, Dad, but probably not too late. They all have to work on Monday."

"Okay. Bye Lisa."

"Bye Dad." Lisa was glad to finally see her dad pull out of their driveway. She ran upstairs to change into her biker garb, but was careful not to put on her jacket that displayed the Skull & Cross colors. She did not want Jess or Jess' family to see it. She waited anxiously downstairs for Mickey.

Jess' mother and step father were trying to give her all the good advice they had to offer about camping when the phone rang. Harvey said, "It's for you, Jess."

"Thanks. Hello. Oh! Hi, Toby," she was saying as she picked up the phone and went into the kitchen with it.

The few precious telephone conversations Chad and Jess had shared through the week had Chad fearing that Lisa was trying to recruit Jess without her knowing of it. If this was true Chad knew what must lay ahead for Jess if she went with Lisa for the weekend. He wanted to prevent her from going. He would simply talk her into staying home and waiting for him to call instead of going with Lisa. He wouldn't be able to make that call later but he would save Jess from the gang stuff that Lisa probably was getting her into. He had nearly told her several times that he was going; but then if she was with this gang, he couldn't risk blowing his cover. If she wasn't, then he would have to make it up to her sometime after the bust. But for now, he could only think of saving her.

"Listen, Renee just called, she said her plans may have been postponed until next weekend. If they are that means Heidi won't be coming over until then. I know this is a bit premature, but I hoped to catch you before you left for your camping trip with Lisa. Renee is supposed to call me back in a few minutes to let me know for sure. Are you following me?"

"So far."

"I was thinking that if she calls before you leave, and she isn't bringing Heidi with her, then maybe you would not go with Lisa this weekend. You could always go camping with her another time. What do you say? I mean, I know this is short notice and all. But well…"

"I don't know…I'm waiting on Lisa and her cousin now. I just don't know what to do for sure."

"Jess, if you had rather go camping, then go camping. I will only be disappointed that you are not going to spend this weekend with me. If you don't go camping then Lisa will be disappointed. So who had you rather disappoint?" He knew he was probably setting himself up for a hurt, but saving her from what possibly awaited ahead comforted him. If he could do it, and if she changed her mind about going, then he would definitely be sure she was not in with the gang.

"I don't know. Give me some time to think about that one. I mean I would probably disappoint Lisa first. But hers is a for sure thing and yours is a maybe. I know I don't want to be sitting at home this weekend. Maybe even if Heidi does come over, this might be as good a time as any to meet her."

None of this sounded good to Chad especially since there was no Heidi to meet. "Please understand that I do want you to meet Heidi as much as I want her to meet you. But until I go to court, I don't want it said that I even had Heidi around another woman before the divorce, just in case I have a chance at having custody."

"Of course, Toby, I understand."

"Jess, do you really?"

"Yes, I really do. Call me back when she calls to let you know. If she has called before Lisa shows up here, then I'll cancel my plans with her. Okay?"

"That's great. Let me get off this phone until she calls."

"Bye, Toby."

"Bye, Beautiful." Chad had to think of what to do and he needed to time it just right to make that call. He didn't want to hang up and call her right back, she might get suspicious about something. No, he would wait for a little bit.

Jess' head was spinning a little after that conversation. She explained the new plans to her mother and Harvey.

"When it rains it pours. You were sitting at home all the time with nothing much to do. And now all of a sudden, it looks like we're going to have to put a bouncer at the front door." As Harvey said this they all laughed.

CHAPTER ELEVEN

Chad was being very impatient as he was waiting to make his call. He decided to put the phone close to the tub in case she decided to call him while he was taking his shower. He really didn't want her to be a victim of Lisa's. Chad knew what went on at a biker's annual convention, and he knew he did not want Jess there. Just as he was dressing after his shower, Kyle knocked on his door.

"Hey, Kyle. Come on in."

"Here, man, I brought dinner."

"Thanks, I could stand a little something in my stomach."

"You seem uptight, Chad. What's up? Has the Chief called or something?"

"Or something."

"What's up?"

"I called Jess to see if she had left yet for her camping trip with Lisa."

"Has she?"

"No, but I need to figure out a way to stop her from going. I'm almost sure that she is being blindly recruited."

"What's Lisa getting her into?"

"I don't know for sure. But you know all those stories that Rex and Shelly told us about what happens to the recruits. I think it all stinks."

"Man, you really are falling for this chick aren't you?"

"Yeah, I guess so." Chad was chewing his last bite of sandwich.

"How long has it been since you called Jess?"

"Not long ago."

"You know you can't tell her anything about who you really are yet. Don't you?"

"Yeah, yeah, I know. I just hope that when I tell her, if I get a chance to tell her, that she will care enough for me to understand. And forgive me for lying to her." His frustrations were about to get to him.

Just then the phone rang, "Hello."

"Daniels, this is Chief Green. Everything has been taken care of until Sunday. Penny is keeping an eye on Styles to make sure he leaves on time. Call Grisham and—"

"He's here, sir." He wanted to get the Chief off the phone so he could call Jess.

"Good. Tell him to get some rest 'til Sunday. Bye."

"Thanks, Chief. Bye."

"What is it, Chad?"

"Just a minute. I have to call Jess first to see if I can catch her. It's nearly seven now. She's probably left already. I hope I'm not too late. Then there's something I need for you to do for me. I'll tell you about it in a minute," Chad was saying as he was dialing the number.

"You got the stuff, man?" asked Mickey to some drug dealer.

"Yeah, man, everything you need is right here." Mickey gave him the cash for the drugs. They wanted to be stocked up before they left Memphis.

"Mickey, it's 6:30, I hope Jess doesn't back out on me. If we don't hurry up, she just might do that, and if she does that, you know better than I do what will happen to me."

"Yeah, and it may not look too good for me, either. That Zack can be a real S.O.B. sometimes, can't he?"

"You ain't lying. Did you get the right stuff?"

"Yeah, I think so."

"Come on, Mickey, you better know so. If you don't have the stuff we need to knock her out with, then I think we will have a problem."

"Look, Lisa, you just get her to drink one beer and I'll do the rest." They drove into Southaven.

"Okay, look, turn here. Then take the third right and keep going until I tell you where to turn next..." Lisa continued giving Mickey the directions to Jess' mom's house.

"Mama, it looks like I might not be going anywhere after all."

"Honey, don't give up so easy. It's not seven yet. They're not even late."

"You're right."

About this time Mickey's van was pulling into the driveway. Lisa got out and rang the doorbell. Jess answered the door.

"I was beginning to think you weren't coming."

"Hi, Mrs. Mitchell."

"Hi, Lisa."

"Bye, Mrs. Mitchell."

"Bye, Lisa."

"It's not seven yet. We made it, even though Mickey got tied up doing something. God only knows what. Are you ready?"

Taking one last look at the phone she hesitated and said, "Yeah, let's go. Bye Mama, tell Harvey, Kara and Bryant I said bye and that I love them. I'll see you some time Sunday."

"Okay, bye. You have a good time and ya'll try to be safe."

Jess and Lisa got in the van.

"Jess, this is Mickey, my cousin. Mickey, this is Jess." They exchanged brief hellos while pulling out of the driveway.

Jess couldn't hear the phone ringing...It was Chad.

Jess was checking out Mickey's van. Even while Mickey drove he was checking out Jess through his rearview mirror. She was sitting on the floor, noticing the shag carpet that seemed to be everywhere. All this red didn't make her feel too safe, for some reason. She was thinking that he could maybe have put in a brown or beige color instead of red. Lisa climbed in the back of the van where the double bed was. It even had a fur cover over it, but at least it was a beige color and not red.

"Come back here, Jess, and tell me all about your date with Toby." Lisa had said.

"All right."

"I've been waiting all week to hear this story. So don't leave out any details." Lisa really was not that interested in Jess' date with Toby. She was just trying to get her ready for what would happen later...She hoped.

"Oh, Lisa it was better than I had hoped for."

"You mean you slept with him?"

"No! I did not. And he really didn't even pressure me the way most guys do."

"Maybe he's after something else."

"I hope so. I mean I hope it's a relationship."

"Do you think you are ready for one?"

"Yeah, I think so."

"Hey, Mickey, put in some Alice Cooper." Lisa yelled up towards the front of the van. She opened up the cooler and took out two Millers, popped the top on one and handed it to Jess.

"Come on, Jess, drink a beer. It will make you feel good."

"I really don't think I want one right now." Jess handed the beer back to Lisa.

Lisa carried the beer to Mickey. She was trying not to let Jess see her pop the top on the un-opened can and then trade it with the one that Mickey had just slipped a Quaalude into. "Here, Mickey, want a beer?"

"No thanks, I've got one." He said as he switched the cans. Lisa came to the back of the van again.

"Here, Jess, you really do need to unwind. Just one beer won't hurt you. It will only relax you and it is going to be a long ride. Besides, I've already opened it for Mickey and he has one. I can't sit here with two opened cans and drink them both before they get hot."

"Okay, if you insist—but just one. Say, where does this Dave fellow live?"

"I don't know, somewhere in Frasier."

Jess leaned back onto some big throw pillows. "Now, tell me about your date with Toby."

Jess began telling Lisa again how wonderful Toby was the night of their date. The two girls sat in the back talking and laughing for a little while. When Jess began feeling groggy, she couldn't believe that one beer made her feel this way.

"Wow. I guess not drinking very often sure makes the effects it can have on you a lot stronger."

"What do you mean?" Lisa knew very well what was happening to Jess.

"I don't know, man, I feel funny. If I didn't know you any better I'd think you put something in my drink." Jess was laughing as she was slurring her words.

Lisa was feeling pleased with herself. But she wanted to get at least one more beer and 'lude down Jess before she fell asleep. Lisa wanted to be sure that Jess would not be aware of Dave's presence later on.

"I love beer. Don't you, Jess? It sure can make you feel good and forget about anything that you don't want to remember."

"Yeah, I guess you right; this is just what I needed. I mean, you're right." Jess was laughing and being silly now. She was doing all she could to stay awake. After all it would be rude to fall asleep before she even met her so called date. *Now, where did that thought come from? He's not my date. I know I made that clear. Or, at least I think I did.* Jess sat her can down and asked Mickey to stop at a gas station. He did and he filled up with gas. As the two girls went to the rest room, Lisa nodded to Mickey and he understood. He switched Jess' can with a new one containing another 'lude.

Back in the van Lisa rolled a joint and began toking on it. "Here, Jess, want to try it?"

"No, I don't think so, Lisa. I don't need that stuff. I think I feel pretty good without it."

Mickey had been watching in his mirror whenever possible to see how far along things were progressing. He was purposefully driving around Memphis before going into Frasier to pick up Dave. He wanted to make sure Jess would be ready for Dave and hopefully even himself.

"Lisa, bring me a joint." Mickey hollered back at her.

"Sure, man, just let me roll you one first." Lisa gave Jess the lit joint to hold while she rolled one for Mickey, hoping she would smoke it. "I think she's ready, Mickey. Why don't you go by and pick up Dave now." Lisa was speaking softly to Mickey so Jess would not hear her.

"Sure chick. I gotta hand it to you. You sure do know how to pick 'em."

"I'm as good as in, cuz."

CHAPTER TWELVE

L isa went to the back of the van. "Say, when do we pick up Toby?"

"You mean Dave, don't you?"

"Yeah, Dave."

"Mickey just told me that's where we're going right now."

"Well, it took us long enough. What time is it, anyway?"

"It's getting close to ten."

"Ten! What have we been doing? Riding around?"

"Yeah, Dave had to work tonight, so we just decided to ride around and get high 'til he got off work. He got off at nine. So about the time we get there, he will be home and changed and ready to go."

This was all a lie. Dave had been waiting impatiently at home for several hours for them to come and pick him up. But he knew the plan well and knew it had to work. This was the biggest event of the year for bikers. He could not wait to see this chick that everyone was talking about, and to think that he would be the first this time. He was remembering last year when he had to be the last one. Man he didn't want to do that again. Even for a dirty biker, filth had a limit. He looked down at his green patch that he'd earned. That's why he would get to be first this year. Mickey's van pulled up out in front of his house. Ah! The moment was here. Dave just couldn't wait. He was out the door before Mickey even put it in park.

Jess meant to climb up towards the front of the van to get a better look at him in the beam of the headlights. But her legs would only allow her to kneel. She was able only to see him briefly before he opened the door of the van. He appeared to be tall. But it was a little hard for Jess to tell for sure. The door swung open.

"Yep, he's tall," Jess unknowingly said out loud.

"Hi," Dave said.

"Jess, this is Dave. Dave, Jess." Lisa said.

"Excuse me, if I don't get up," Jess was weaving as she was trying to extend her hand and compose herself in a proper manor. "Hi. I'm Jess Talbot." Dave took her hand as he shut the door behind himself. "I usually don't drink, so I guess I couldn't hold down my one little beer. I'm sorry I don't think I will be a very good date for you." *There's that word again. I've got to stop saying that word, 'date.' I hope he knows that I'm not his date.*

Dave began to help Jess get up onto the bed in the van. He leaned her back up against the pillows and tried to make her feel comfortable. Jess didn't like what he was doing, but she was too out of it by now to say anything. Dave removed his hands from around her and sat not too close to her and was just looking her over. "Don't worry,"

He said. "I don't take advantage of women." Dave was lying through his teeth. But he was just trying to get Jess relaxed again.

What's he saying? Jess was thinking, but she couldn't comprehend anything by now and with that she closed her eyes.

Dave slipped up to the front of the van, taking one last look back at Jess before speaking to Lisa and Mickey. "Jess," he called back to her to see if she could hear him. There was no response, nevertheless, Dave decided he had better keep it down to a whisper. "Lisa, I think you've outdid yourself."

"I knew everyone would want her."

"I can't wait for my turn," said Mickey.

"Thanks, Lisa. I'll do you a favor later," said Dave.

"Maybe she's ready." He made his way to the back of the van where the unconscious, vulnerable Jess was laying. He placed his hand on her leg. No protesting there, so he began moving it farther up her thigh. Oh, yeah! She was ready. Dave cuddled in a little closer. He tossed his empty beer can on the floor. He lifted her nearly empty beer can out of her hand and secured it in-between the wall of the van and the bed mattress.

Lisa and Mickey stole glances from time to time.

—◌◌◌—

Kyle and Chad were sitting in Chad's living room. Chad had just explained his fears to Kyle. And how he would do all he could to warn Jess of the plot against her. He knew that he had to do this without jeopardizing his position with the Skull & Cross. Kyle spoke of his feelings about the whole situation. He had not been convinced as of yet that Jess was as naïve as Chad thought.

"It's nearly time for me to go, Kyle." Just then there was a knock at the door. Chad looked through the peep hole. "It's Penny. Kyle you can stay here if you want, man, but I got to go."

"Cool. Hey, man, don't worry. I'm sure you'll run into her."

Chad looked through his peep hole again. "It's Penny."

"You said that."

"Come on in. What's up?"

Penny moved over to the wing back chair and took a seat.

"What are you doing here, Kyle?" asked Penny even though she was hoping to find him here.

Kyle said nothing at all because Chad was so anxious to get going. "They are meeting at Zack's at midnight and leaving out from there, so I got to go now."

"Let me remind you, Styles has told Zack that you'll be riding with them, and that you are interested in seeing how smooth this transaction will go down in case you're interested in a purchase in the future from his provider," said Penny.

"That's about the sum of it," Chad replied.

Penny continued, "Did you also know that Styles has told us the exchange will take place on a shipping dock off of Riverside Drive, he just has to let us know the ETA and exact dock...I hope he comes through for us on Sunday."

"Listen, I'd love to stay and chat all night, but I gotta go."

"Yeah, to rescue a princess. He's gonna be her knight in shining armor," Kyle said.

"Yeah, I hope so. Maybe that part will make Jess more understanding to my lies. I better go." And with that he left.

"I guess, I'd better be leaving, too. I just wanted to see him off."

"Why don't you stay for a while and keep me company. I'll probably be up for a while worrying about Chad and wishing I were going along for the excitement."

"If you're sure you don't mind." She liked that idea a great deal.

"I don't mind."

CHAPTER THIRTEEN

Jess was beginning to wake up. Lisa could hear her moans, so she began to pick herself up off of the carpeted floor. She sat upon the bed close to Jess.

"Hey, are you all right?"

"O-O-O-H-H!" exclaimed Jess.

"What's going on Jess? Are you feeling okay?" She was testing to see how much Jess remembered.

Dave was sitting up front with Mickey.

"I don't know. What happened last night?" She was grabbing her head and trying to sit up.

"Take it easy. You really tied one on last night."

"Last night." She was trying to remember what did happen last night but knew nothing, except she was very sore. She rubbed her neck and realized that it felt bruised. Not only that but she was naked under a blanket. "Lisa! Where are my clothes?" she whispered.

"I don't know. Here, let me help you find them."

"You do it... I don't feel much like moving."

Lisa gathered up all of her clothes and was swinging her panties around on her finger.

Jess snatched them out of her hand and began to get dressed under the covers. "What happened to me last night, Lisa?"

"Jess, I was shocked! I didn't know you'd really go as far as you did on just two beers."

"Two? I only had one. Right?"

"No. It was two, you wanted another one so Dave gave it to you. Don't you remember?"

"No...I don't remember much of anything after that one, first one. I'm sure it was something else. Someone must have put something in my drink last night?"

"Jess, you know me better than that. I'm shocked that you would even think such a thing."

"Dave. What about Dave?"

"What about Dave? You mean did he put something in your beer? I don't think so."

"That too. But I mean did he...did I...?"

"Yes, he did and yes, you did."

"Oh, man. I-I-I-I think I'm going to be sick."

"Here." Lisa took some nearly melted ice cubes out of the chest and wrapped them in a piece of cloth. "Here, put this on your head." Lisa was holding the cloth on Jess' head.

Jess felt uneasy about all this. "Thanks. I'll do it myself."

Lisa left Jess to her thoughts and made her way up front on her knees in between the two seats.

Jess leaned back on the pillows, watching for road signs to get her bearings on where they were. She had been lying there for some time trying to remember what took place last night or how she even let it happen. She was sore, embarrassed, and ashamed. She felt like crying.

The sun would be coming up soon. She could see that it was nearly daybreak. Mickey was asleep in the passenger's seat and Dave was driving. From time to time he would look back at her through the rearview mirror. Jess couldn't see his face very clearly but from what she could see of him, he was gross. She began to look outside again not believing what she had done the night before. What had she done?

While staring out the window, she finally focused in on a group of motorcycles that had been following them for some time now. There still wasn't enough daylight to see what they looked like. Dave kept looking back at her and giving her disgusting kiss signs with his lips through the mirror. This was making Jess feel even more sick. "Why am I here?"

"What was that, Jess?" Lisa asked as she made her way back to the rear of the van.

"Lisa, how far to the next stop? I need to go to the bathroom."

"Just a few miles to Nashville. We'll stop there and have breakfast."

The thought of food was making Jess very sick to her stomach. "Lisa?"

"Yeah."

"Those motorcycles back there have been following us all morning. You think they're going to the same place we are?"

Lisa knew that they would all be pulling off at the next exit together. She would have to break the news to her somehow and sometime. She guessed that now was as good as any. "Yeah, Jess, they're part of a gang. But, it's okay, they are just following along with us. You know—safety in numbers."

"What gang?" Jess said while shaking her head negatively.

"The Skull & Cross gang."

"How do you know all this?"

"Mickey was telling me this last night. I don't think you have anything to worry about."

"I'm not so sure."

Dave was ready to rescue Lisa. "Lisa come up here and look on the map. I think the next exit is the one we want. We don't want to get off on one that will be too hard to get back onto the freeway from."

Jess found her brush and mirror in her purse. She was shocked when she noticed all the hickey marks and bruises. *Why did I come? How can I get out of this? What am I doing here?*

Mickey woke up as they were exiting the freeway.

Jess looked back to see if those motorcycles were going to exit also. They did.

Dave pulled up to a Pancake House. The four of them got out of the van. As quickly as Jess could, she fled for the bathroom. The commode could not have come any quicker. When she finished puking her guts out, she cleaned herself up with some paper towels. Jess was feeling better, until she came out of the bathroom and saw all those bikers sitting around ordering breakfast. She didn't want anyone to see her with all those bruises and marks all over her body and she sure didn't want to be seen with any of these thugs. And then, she couldn't believe her eyes; she even had to close them and look again. There he was, Toby. She purposefully would not look his way when she passed him by.

Chad never took his eyes off of her. She looked horrible. Either she was part of them, and he wanted nothing more to ever do with her and looked forward to busting her or worse, it had already begun. He didn't know whether to fume or what? His emotions were confused. If it had begun he couldn't do anything because in doing so, he would blow his cover.

"Don't even think about it," said a Skull & Cross member noticing the look in Chad's eyes.

Jess, confused, heard Toby ask, "Man, where'd you find a chick like that?" Chad was trying to smooth over the look he had given. He couldn't do anything to blow his cover. He was finding it hard to do since he saw how spent Jess looked, and she wouldn't even look at him. What must she think of him? That he was one of them? That he would use her just like it looked like someone already had? He was trying to keep his cool. He needed a chance to talk to her. It was all he could do to not grab her and leave. He was so confused.

Jess found the booth Lisa, Mickey, and Dave were sitting in. She reluctantly sat there with them. This was the first time she had really gotten a good look at Dave. He was sitting across from her. He was more than gross; he was almost hideous. Of course right now, everything was hideous. The only thing Jess wanted was orange juice.

She couldn't help but notice all the stares they were getting from the normal looking people. She wanted to scream out that she was not a part of these people or better yet, animals. And why is Lisa having anything to do with them? Has she lost her mind?

All of the other members looked like something that had walked right out of the gutter. Except Toby, not because she really had liked him before this, but the fact that he was clean and looked as if he had showered and shaved. He was wearing a white T-shirt and jeans. Although his shirt did have a picture of a great big motorcycle on it, he was clean. To Jess it didn't even look like a Harley, but what did she know for sure? Nothing, at this point.

Jess looked down at her partially visible breast only to see all the blood-sucked markings. She looked up and all around at the people still staring. She must look to them the way those grungy bikers look to her. She couldn't bear this thought. She tried to dismiss it. She was nearly in tears. And then, why is Toby here? What part did he play in all this? This made her want to cry even more. What must he think of her, the way she looked? It didn't matter anymore to her what he must think, if he wanted this kind of lifestyle she wanted no part of him.

"Come on, it's time to go," said Dave as he took her elbow to escort her out of the restaurant. Jess did not want to do anything to upset him. She didn't know for sure what she should do. But one thing was for sure, she would do anything and everything she could to get back home safely and in one piece.

Why did Toby, call me and lie to me like that? Was it because he knew this whole time that he was going and he didn't want me to come, but if not, then why not? She was so confused and mad at him right now. Then again, if he had called me I wouldn't be in this mess.

As soon as they were outside, Jess quickly broke away from Dave. She found Lisa and moved a little closer to her. Mickey got in on the driver's side of the van, Dave got in up front, and Jess began to get into the back of the van when she noticed eight, vulture-like eyes in there looking at her.

Jess turned to see Lisa, now wearing a biker vest, getting onto the back of a bike. Without hesitation, Jess found a lone biker next to Lisa. "Can I ride with you?" Jess was asking this lone biker. She figured that with him being so skinny that if he gave her any trouble she might be able to handle herself, although, it all made her frighteningly sick. Lisa, and Toby, had some nerve, doing her that way.

"Sure chick. Get on." So, she did. She and the lone biker, Stoney, pulled out first and next to them was Lisa and Styles. Much to her disgusting surprise, Toby pulled out with them.

CHAPTER FOURTEEN

Chad had had to choose his job or Jess. He knew that Stoney was Styles' friend and that Stoney had no idea that Styles was using him as a cover to make himself look better to his gang. It had also been made clear that when the bust went down that Stoney and Styles were to be set free. Chad chose his job, knowing that otherwise he may go to jail, and hoped that Stoney would stay with Styles.

"What's your name?"

"Jess," she was so scared. She was shaking. "What's yours?"

"They call me Boney Stoney. You can just call me Stoney."

"I think this is my first time on a Harley, Stoney."

"Well, we're going to see some beautiful country today. Just sit back and enjoy the ride. Have you ever been to a biker's convention?"

"No. Is it anything like where we're going?"

"And where might that be?"

"To a motocross race." She didn't like his laughter after her comment.

This chick has a body that won't quit. But can she really be this naïve? After last night has she not figured it all out yet? Stoney just couldn't believe anyone could be so stupid.

"What's so funny, Stoney?"

"Nothing, I think we're in for a lot of fun today."

"I could use something good to cheer me up."

Tired of the yelling going on between them because of the wind, Jess leaned back on the sissy bar and was trying to forget about last night and just enjoy the scenery for a while. She was safe for the moment. Even if they were to have a wreck, surely she would be rescued from whatever lay ahead. No, she would not think about it right now; she would try to enjoy this ride as best as her sore body would let her.

—◦◦◦—

"Chief, may I come in?"

"Come on in here, Grisham. I thought I told you to take the day off."

"Yes sir. You did but I have nothing else I'd rather be doing than working on this case."

"Shh, Shh," Chief Green said as he closed the door. "Have you had doughnuts yet?"

"No, sir. I got up and came on in first thing."

"Let's go somewhere, so we can talk and have doughnuts. Norma, we're going out for doughnuts. Hold all my calls." Chief Green and Kyle Grisham left the office to go for breakfast.

"Yes sir, Chief. I'll have some fresh coffee waiting on you," Green's secretary, Norma Jenkins, told him. She had been his secretary for fourteen years now. Norma was the only one that he trusted with everything and anything, sometimes he even trusted her more than he trusted his own wife.

———⋙ᴐ∕∂∕ᴐ⋘———

After being on the road for about an hour, Boney Stoney pulled over to the side shoulder.

"What are we stopping for?"

"To smoke. Can't smoke and ride too."

"Oh."

All five got off their bikes to stretch a bit. Jess was now faced with being in a small group of five, Toby being one of them. She couldn't figure out why Toby was there. Little did she know that he was not going to leave Styles at this point, nor why.

"So, you're Jess," Styles was saying.

"Yeah, that's me," She still felt bad about how she must look, especially to a biker. She sure didn't want to give him the wrong impression.

While Lisa, Styles, and Stoney were smoking a cigarette, they were also smoking weed. Chad and Jess smoked neither.

"Here, Jess," Stoney was trying to get her to smoke with them. He wanted to get her stoned.

"No, thank you."

"This ain't just no ordinary weed, man. This is Jamaican laced with coke." He talked through his teeth while holding his breath and sucking in more air at intervals, and waving it in her face.

"No. No, thank you. I don't want that either. Besides, do you think it's safe to be on a bike while on that stuff?"

"I do it all the time. Am I still here?" Stoney said.

He had a point there; nevertheless, she didn't like it. As she sat there listening to the others engage in conversations she knew nothing about, she noticed that Toby didn't have a fowl mouth like the others, including Lisa. He had not said much though and had said nothing to her. This made her even more mad at him. It didn't matter if he never spoke to her, she would never speak to him again.

"How much farther?" Jess asked no one in particular. Not even wanting to talk to Lisa anymore.

"We ought to be just outside of Bowling Green close to lunch time." Chad said, staring at Jess the whole time trying to get her to read what was in his eyes and on his mind.

He speaks. Jess thought as she glared at him.

"Come on guys, we need to get on the road. You don't want to let Zack get there before you do." Chad said.

"Hey man, he's right," said Styles. "Let's go." They all mounted up and road off.

"Half a dozen doughnuts and two coffees," Green said. He and Grisham had entered a little greasy spoon restaurant on Madison Avenue, near the square.

"Grisham, you seem to have something on your mind. What's up?"

"There is something I need to talk to you about, the girl that I was casing out, Lisa. Chad and I have good reason to believe that she is a recruiter for the Skull & Cross."

"Yeah, yeah, I think you may have mentioned it before."

"Well, sir, Chad wanted me to be sure and request that you see to it that this Jess Talbot chick, that is with them, not get busted tomorrow."

"Okay and why not?"

"Sir, she is the one we believe is being recruited by Lisa for their gang."

"Go on."

"We don't think she even knows why she's there."

"That's sad."

"Yes, sir, but that's what biker gangs do, sir."

"I know, Grisham. I know. Those dirty bikers."

"Exactly, sir."

"Don't worry, Grisham. If it turns out that she has no knowledge of what's happening to her, she'll be all right. I promise."

Jean and Mae were gathered together with a few more ladies from their church and community at a prayer room in the back, as they did every Saturday morning at this same time. Prayer requests were made known and praise reports were given. These women began to pray for each need. Jess was also lifted up in prayer for her safety, and a safe return from her camping trip. It was usually two to three hours that these women remained in intercessory prayer. They were serious and knew how to reach God and believed him for every request. This was an awesome place to be and be thought about. To be lifted up before the very throne of God keep a lot of people alive. Would it work for Jess today?

CHAPTER FIFTEEN

There it is, the Bowling Green exit. Her anticipation was building by the moment, not knowing what was ahead for her. All she knew was that it was not where she wanted to be, now or ever. As soon as they were off the interstate, they pulled into a steak and breakfast place to take a break and grab a bite to eat. Jess and Lisa headed off toward the restroom.

"Lisa, I still don't really understand why you didn't tell me about this gang member business."

"Would you have come if I did?"

"No, I would not."

"Look, Jess, I did this for you. It's the only way I know how to try and make you happy for a change. I only wanted to see you get out and have some fun. I'm only trying to be a friend." Lisa knew better than to tell her the truth just yet. There was still enough road between them and the park for Jess to try and get away, especially with Toby so nearby. And with what happened last night in the van she knew that everything was working out toward her getting her initiation. She would do whatever it took to get that initiation.

"Lisa, what happened last night in the van?"

"Jess, I'd say you made Dave a happy man last night."

"I mean, why did that happen?"

"What do you mean? You should have seen yourself. You were enjoying every minute of it." Lisa didn't bother to tell her what had happened to her, after Dave.

"I keep thinking that my body is telling me that more than being with Dave went on. I know, if I keep thinking about it; eventually, I'll remember or figure it out." But it was also something she wanted to forget.

"I don't know exactly what you're trying to figure out. But I do know that you were really hot last night."

"What do you mean by that?"

"That's just what Dave kept saying." And Mickey, but she wouldn't tell her that. Lisa was trying to be convincing, she surely didn't want Jess to know the truth. The girls left the bathroom.

"I need to call home," Jess said.

"Why?" Lisa was afraid that she would be trying to go home.

"I promised Harvey I would call when I made it to Bowling Green."

"Oh."

Jess made her call. Lisa hung around the corner, just out of Jess's view.

"Hello."

"Hi. Harvey this is Jess. I made it okay."

"Are you having fun yet?"

"Well, it's been enlightening. I'll tell you all about it when I get home."

"Okay. Call us if you need us."

"Okay. I will. I know that Mama is at her prayer meeting. Tell her I love her and to keep praying for me, and I love you, too. I'm doing fine and I will see you both tomorrow. Bye." She hung up before Harvey even had time to be heard.

"Bye, Sugar." He said as he hung up the dead phone.

Jess was not about to tell him her fears. She knew that they couldn't really afford to drive all the way to Kentucky. And she didn't want them sitting at home worrying about her. No, she was a grown woman now and she would handle this the best way possible. She may even be worrying over nothing. After all the worst was over; she had made her mistake with Dave and now was out of it. At least believing this was comforting her a bit.

When Jess had entered the restaurant area, Stoney stood up to let her sit in the booth with him. Lisa was then sitting directly across from her next to Styles. In the booth behind Jess, Chad sat alone. They were the only ones in the restaurant eating lunch this early. Jess decided she needed to act cool with all of this if she was to learn anything; it was her best defense right now. So, she began chatting with them all, except Toby, she was laughing making everyone feel comfortable around her. The whole time this was making her sick, but she couldn't let them know this.

What is she doing? Thought Chad confused.

"I'm curious, Stoney, what are all those patches for?"

"Jess!" exclaimed Lisa in astonishment.

"I figure that the only way I will learn anything about bikers is if I ask questions. I might like to join myself." Of course, she had no intentions of joining any biker gang; she had ulterior motives.

"It's okay, Lisa," said Stoney. "They each have a meaning."

"So, what do they mean?"

"This one,"—pointing to a red one—"means that I had to stab someone to earn it. That's why it's red."

Jess laughed at his remark, trying to fit in, "You mean, you killed someone?"

"No, I just stabbed them."

"What does this blue one mean?" She was gently caressing the blue triangle patch located on his left pocket as she purposefully leaned closer brushing next to his body.

He quickly placed his arm around her, "I had to rob a store to earn that one." He then proceeded to tell her about each patch.

"Earn them? Like boy scouts?" He laughed at this. She flirted with him the whole time. "So are they like dare patches?"

They were all laughing now, except Chad. He just sat back there, fuming quietly and listening.

"Yeah, I guess you could call it that. But that's not what we call it."

"Okay, then what do you call it?"

"They mean rank."

"Rank?" She was smiling at him and playing dumb.

"Yeah, like how many more patches you have earned, then that's how much rank you have."

Counting the number of patches she could see, "You've earned at least seven. Does that mean you have a lot of rank or a little? I mean, if I'm going to be with someone, I sure want him to have a lot of rank."

Chad was thinking either this chick has gone crazy, or she's very clever.

Stoney kind of laughingly said, "No, I don't have a lot, that's for sure. I haven't even been initiated yet. I had to earn all these patches before I could even begin initiation."

"So, how do you get initiated?"

"You sure do ask a lot of questions," Lisa said. She and Styles had just been listening and laughing with them at most of her questions and his answers, until now.

Jess just gave her a funny look and said nothing.

"I'm here to earn my green patch." Stoney said.

"How do you do that?" She teased his vest with her finger.

"It's not how I do it. It's what I do."

"Or who you do it with." Styles said as he laughed. Styles had no idea that Chad knew Jess and did not want her there. Nor could Chad tell him anything about it, at this point. He was doing his best to hide his anger, and how much he wanted to get these two guys. If only he could tell Jess.

"Well, don't keep me in suspense. Tell me, what do you do?" She was intentionally turning him on.

He squirmed a little in his seat, "All of the gang members take a chick, you know, one that is on her monthly or has just come off one, and they have their way with her, anything they want to do. Then I have breakfast, lunch, or call it what you want, depends on what time they're done with her. Understand?"

It took a few minutes for Jess to take this in. She could not fathom that something so horrible would actually be done to a person or that anyone would even dare participate to earn a "Green" patch. This was something you may have read in a book or seen on TV but not in real life. She no longer could laugh at this, suddenly she withdrew her hand from his jacket and sat up straight in her seat, the atmosphere changed. "Ugh, that's the most sickening thing, I've ever heard. How can you stand to do that? That is gross of all grosses." She had heard enough. She turned her head away at this. She could not believe what she was hearing. She caught a glimpse of Lisa sinking down in her seat a little, as if she were trying to hide away.

Stoney and Styles were laughing at her.

Wait a minute. She was thinking but not speaking. I fit that description. She knew all too well that Lisa knew she had just come off her period. She had slept with Dave already, and maybe now she had even slept with Mickey. *Maybe that explains why my body feels the way it does.* She felt she had not truly slept with anyone. *No, I've been raped. Surely, Lisa would not let them do this to me. Or would she?* Jess was now staring hard at Lisa. *Maybe she did put something in my drink.*

Lisa continued to sink lower, under the table almost. Jess' eyes seemed to bore right through her. They would have to kill her first, before she let anything like that happen to her. They all remained quiet from that point on.

So much was going on in Jess' mind right now. She couldn't help but think there was a possibility that she was here to help Stoney earn his green patch. She knew that she would never let that happen to her. But how could she prevent it? Why hadn't Toby said anything? She knew now that whatever feelings she thought she had for him were for sure gone. *What was the date we had the other night truly about? Just so he could go ahead and be one of those others that Stoney was talking about? Of course, it must have been. Why else would he be here with a gang, the same one that apparently Lisa belongs to. This whole thing has been a plot from the beginning. Lisa knew Toby all this time and she acted like she had just met him.* Jess was really boiling inside and sick at the same time. She knew now that she was truly on her own.

"Jess…" Stoney was saying.

She came out of her thoughts for the moment to see them all standing there waiting on her to get up, even Toby. This made her sick and enraged with hatred. She got up and left with them, reluctantly.

Jess rode with Stoney again.

Jess had come up with a plan. *As soon as we come into town I will jump off this bike and run into a store and yell for help.* At this point, she felt that would give her a chance of surviving.

CHAPTER SIXTEEN

I t was only about a twenty-minute ride that seemed forever, through some beautiful country to get to the town of Bowling Green. Jess was surprised that she could even take her mind off of her situation long enough to notice. It was like some kind of therapy for her, smelling the freshness of the trees and the clear country air. Not like the sweltering asphalt odors of the city.

Jess couldn't believe her eyes as they came into Bowling Green. Here it was on a Saturday morning around eleven-thirty or so. Every store front right down on Main Street was boarded up, every home that was anywhere near that area was boarded up. This was not an abandoned town; that was easy to tell. Everything was too well kept. The people knew what was coming to their precious, quiet little town that weekend, so they were either not there or in good hiding. Any thoughts she had earlier of jumping off the bike and running into a store for help were gone.

Even more frightening were the number of bikers raising cane there in the streets. The bikers at that main square were as thick as matches in a match box. Jess had never in her life seen anything like it, not even on TV. TV hadn't even come close to having anything like this on it, nor had any books that she had read. Come to think about it, she had not read any books about biker stories. She had heard things about the Hell's Angels, but that was all. Usually on TV they may have had one large group of bikers to ride into a town and bust it up, but nothing like this.

They were screaming and hollering obscenities that she would never repeat, anywhere or anytime. They were stripping girls' clothing off of them right there in the streets. Even worse, the girls liked it, encouraged it even. Oh, to be out of here. And out of here she would be, first chance she got.

They rode through the town, turned and headed in a northerly direction. They rode maybe five minutes away from all the wild commotion downtown and pulled off to the side of the road into a small pasture area filled with more bikers, a couple of mobile food venders and a few porta potties.

They parked their bikes and got off. "I thought you said there would be a camping ground area, carnival rides, and a motocross race?" Jess angrily directed this question to Lisa.

"I did, Jess. This is not the place. We'll go there in a little while."

"What are we doing here?" Her anger was building.

Lisa sighed. "This is where we purchase the tickets to the camping area. We have to wait on Zack; he's the one with all the money for the tickets."

They all walked over to the top of a little gully under some trees, except for Styles and Chad.

"Why do we have to wait? Why can't we just go now?" Jess protested.

"We have to wait till the president of the gang gets here, and the rest of the gang," Stoney told her.

This place reminded her of the woods near her home where she grew up as a little girl. It was a nice cool shady place where they were waiting. Only they had sat her down just below the top of the gully, so that she couldn't see anybody, and so no one could see her. About twenty minutes of strained silence had passed before someone came over the edge and relieved Stoney.

"Wait, I want to go with you." Jess told Stoney.

He said nothing as he and Lisa walked off. The new guy told her to sit back down and with that he pressed her shoulders down making her sit. During this time Jess was still trying to think of what to do to get out of this mess. Her anger and fear were still showing.

"Man, it's a long line at that stand." Stoney said as he came back holding out cold drinks for everyone.

"Any sign of Zack?" The new guy asked.

"Naw, but there are a few more members here, Zack is about half an hour behind them. You know how he is. Everyone wants to be here before he gets here. We don't want to keep him waiting."

"You got that right. He sure gets upset when he wants to."

"So, who is Zack? Is he this president of your gang?"

"Yeah, he is," said Stoney.

"I wish someone would tell me what's really going on here. Why are there so many bikers here?"

"Jess, you ask too many questions. Why don't you shut up for a while." Stoney told her and he was not speaking in a nice voice, nor was he asking a question.

Jess just sat there for a while but refused to be quiet. "How much longer?" she asked for the umpteenth time, as she tried to stand up and walk away, once again.

Stoney backhanded her. "Shut up, and sit down."

Jess' lip began to trickle a little blood, she wiped it with the back of her hand and her eyes began to sting with tears, but she refused to let them come out. She knew she would have to find a way out of this place.

Just then another biker came walking up with some biker chick. "Zack and the other members are here now. Let's go."

They walked over to Mickey's van. There was another van parked right behind his. There were about fifteen to twenty bikes parked beside the van and a whole other group of bikers were there, including men and women. And right there sitting on his bike at the front of the group was Toby. He still didn't look the part as did the others. Nor did he have any chicks with him.

Chad turned his head to look at Jess as they came closer. He saw the puffed up lip. He wanted to take her and ride off.

Lisa walked over and got on the back of a bike with a biker that Jess had never seen before. Jess started to get on Stoney's bike with him. She felt that that would be okay and much safer than in the van. And heaven forbid she'd ask Toby.

"You can't ride with me," Stoney said, shaking his head no. "You have to ride in the van," shaking his head yes.

She looked in the van. There were about ten grubby, grungy, dirty looking bikers in that van.

"Can I ride with you?" She asked Styles.

"No, you have to ride in the van."

She looked at Lisa.

"You have to ride in the van." Lisa told her.

She again looked in the van. "I am not riding in that van."

"You have to." They all said, almost simultaneously as some of them were making their way towards her.

She couldn't be sure Toby didn't say it, but she thought he said nothing.

"*I AM NOT RIDING IN THAT VAN.*" She shouted. She had no choice and no time but turned suddenly and asked, "Toby, can I ride with you?"

Everyone froze. Chad searched the faces of each biker. If looks could kill, he would have been dead right then. He revved up his engine, "Yeah, get on." His bike was nearly moving before she got on. As soon as his tires hit the pavement, "There's probably going to be a fight. But let's go anyway."

Even though Jess didn't look back, Chad could see them shaking their fists at him through his mirrors. He had done it, he had left Styles, but at least not before he made the connection with the seller. That is what he had been doing while Jess and everyone had been waiting for Zack and the gang. He knew he had to get the information needed for the bust before he could even think about grabbing Jess and fleeing the gang. The Skull

& Cross gang did not know that Styles had ratted, and that he was planning to pull out early in the morning with Toby.

———∽∾∽———

Was he doing her a favor or did he want her all to himself? All she knew for the moment was that she was not in that van.

The traffic would not allow them to move very fast at all. They were only able to take a right with the flow of traffic and move a few feet and then stop. This is the way it was for the next two miles.

It was a beautiful day. Neither of them wore a helmet. They were able to talk freely and not against the wind. Nor did they have to yell at each other in order to be heard.

Jess was the first one to speak. "Thank you." She hated even saying that. She barely even let her body touch his. She was still revolted over having to ride with him.

"You're welcome."

The traffic was moving so slow that Chad kept his feet on the ground more often than not.

Jess just couldn't keep quiet forever. She had to find a way out of all this. "Why did you do it?"

"Do what?"

"Why did you not turn me down like all the others?"

"I'm not like all the others. And, I am not a member of their gang."

"Sure, you're not!"

"No. I belong to a biker's club."

"A biker's club? Yeah, right."

"Yes, a club."

"Club–Gang, what's the difference?"

"We're not a gang. We don't do the things gangs do. We're just a few people who like bikes."

"So, what's the name of *this club*!" she asked sarcastically.

"The Riders, we all don't even ride Harleys."

"I knew your bike looked different. What is it?

Chad laughed at this. "It's a Honda CC, a 1000. It's called the Cadillac of the Hondas."

"It sure is big, and comfortable." Jess was noticing how big Toby's muscles were, and how broad his shoulders were, and remembering how she'd felt being held by him. She just wished all this strength made her feel safe right now. But she still didn't know what his plans were for her. Why is he riding with them? What's his connection with Lisa? She would just use him to get out of there.

"Jess, do you know what was going on back there?"

"Not really. No. I'm not sure." She had her suspicions, but she did not want to accept what she feared.

"You know that green patch that Stoney was talking about earning?"

"Yeah."

"They are going to use you as their guinea pig to help Stoney earn his green patch."

"Oh, no, they're not!"

"That's what their plans are."

"I'll walk right out of this place."

"Jess, look around you. You'll never make it out of here alive by yourself."

She did look around and thought long and hard about everything that was happening before speaking what she finally settled within her heart. "Then...today is the day I will die." She meant every word of it and was truly prepared to die.

She was still overwhelmed by all the bikers. The fact that they were bikers probably wouldn't be so bad to try and make an escape for it, but they all looked so nasty and acted so wild, all except for Toby.

What makes him so different? "And just what do you have to do with all this, Toby?"

"Jess, you've got to trust me on this."

"You talk about trust? What was this calling me bit last night when you knew the whole time that you were coming here."

Chad got a brilliant idea. He thought it out clearly before he spoke it. "Jess, I had every intention of you coming over last night. I called you back, but you had left already, or else I wouldn't be here now, nor would you."

This was giving her something to think about. "Really, so, that's really why you are here?"

"Jess, think about it. If I am not with this gang, why else would I be riding here with them?"

"That's what I'm trying to find out," raising her hands in frustration.

"After your mom said you had left, I knew where you were going, so I talked with Rex and Shelly, some friends of mine that were already coming, and I decided to come too. But only because I knew that you would be here," Chad hated lying to her like this, but he needed her to trust him and stay with him, so he could be sure of her safety. Hopefully, when all this was over, he would be able to explain it all and she would forgive him.

"Why didn't you say something earlier, like in Nashville or this morning at that restaurant?"

Boy, this is really going to help me cover for myself, so far. "Jess, I know that when I took you out the other night, we talked about bikers and such. And I got the impression that you didn't like them, nor wanted to have anything to do with them, so I wasn't really sure where you stood about being here. But when I saw you this morning in Nashville." He paused not really knowing how to put it. There was no nice way to put it. "Well, with all those marks on your body. What was I supposed to think?"

Toby is right. Jess began to think about how it must look to him, her willingly coming here with Lisa. Seeing her with them this morning looking the way she did. Even though she didn't know that she was being tricked. How could he know that she had been lied to?

"I am so ashamed, embarrassed, outraged, and anything else you can think of. I believe they put something in my beer last night. I would never let this happen. *Never.*" She was almost crying.

Chad reached his hand back to pat her knee. "It's okay Jess. I believe you. Them SOBs. Boy, what I'd like to do to them." He was getting so angry his muscles bulged with redness. "This morning at the restaurant, when Stoney was explaining about his green patch, it was then that I began to think that you might not know what was going on. I wanted to snatch you right out of there, but I could tell that you were sore at me and probably wouldn't go. And then you started acting like you wanted to be there. What was that all about?"

"Sore. Sore is not even close. Oh, Toby, I'm sorry. I can see where you would think that I knew what I was doing, especially after the way I acted at the restaurant and was snubbing you so well."

"You must have thought some pretty awful things about me as well. I must have seemed like a jerk to you the whole time."

"Up until now, you did. And back at the restaurant, I was just pretending so I could gather information."

"Whew! I'm glad we got that cleared up."

CHAPTER SEVENTEEN

"Toby, what's next? I don't know what to do now. I do know what I'm not going to do. I am not going to be anybody's guinea pig."

"Jess, I can try to get you out of this if you want me to."

Jess had to think about this. If she said yes, would the same thing happen to her with his club members? Or was he telling her the truth? She wasn't sure if he could be trusted. If he was lying, at least she would be taken by someone that had had a bath. At least this was someone saying they wanted to help her and not hurt her, but what about the other members of his *club*? When it came down to it, what did she have to lose, possibly, the same thing to either group, her life?

"Well, do you?"

"Yes! I'm sorry, yes, of course I do."

"Did you really not know what they were planning to do?"

"No, I really didn't. I know you must think I'm stupid or something."

"A bit naïve, but never stupid. Stupid would be to turn down my offer and go back to their demands."

"I don't know how to thank you for saving my life. And I mean really saving my life, because they would have had to kill me first. I would have died before I let them do that to me."

"And die you would have, if I hadn't been here."

"I sure do owe you a lot for rescuing me."

"Don't thank me yet. It's not over."

"What do you mean?"

"There may be a fight."

"I don't understand gangs. What do you mean?"

"What will happen first is that I will go to the president of my club and see if they will back me up."

"And if they won't?"

"Then I'll do the best I can on my own. But, don't worry they will probably back me up."

On his own! Will he really do that? Is he truly a good guy or am I just a pawn between two gangs so they can prove which gang is the best? Oh, I wish I knew.

"I hope so! I'm sorry I've got you into this mess."

"You didn't get me into anything. I chose to do this myself," he said as he continued to pat her knee.

"You just may turn out to be my knight in shining armor." She surely hoped this was true. But after the lessons in life she was learning this weekend she would take things very slow from now on. Things are not what they seem is what she was beginning to see. And don't trust anyone. But could she trust Toby? She really wanted to. Jess was willing herself to feel much better about Toby. She leaned back and enjoyed the beauty of the landscape of Kentucky, for a moment. She was seeing why it was called the bluegrass state. The countryside was beautiful and full of greenery. This ride to the park was taking longer than it did to get through McKellar Park on a Sunday afternoon. "How far is it?"

"About another mile."

"There sure are a lot of people out here."

"There's more on the inside."

"What's it like?"

"Nothing you've ever seen; I can assure you." He was remembering his first one last year.

"How many of these have you been too?"

"They have three or four a year, a lot smaller than this one. This is only once a year; it's an annual biker's convention."

"An annual biker's convention? I was told I was coming to a motocross race. I can think of someplace else I'd rather be." She was again thinking of being at his place with him. What is this feeling for him? She wasn't ready for all this.

"Yeah, I think I could even enjoy it better if it were under different circumstances."

Now what did he mean by that? Just then they rounded a corner. "Oh, my gosh! Look at all those cops."

"Yeah, they're here for protection."

"Who's?"

"Anyone not on the inside."

Jess was carefully eyeing the vast number of police officers standing nearly an arm's length apart in front of a high chain link fence that separated one side of a beautiful spread of velvet green grass in a wide open space. Off in the distance to the left of the chain link fence, aligned with cops, was a poorly erected barn standing alone, far away from a barbed wire fence. Her gaze swept to an area on the other side that appeared to have a path of a road in front of a tree line going in either direction parallel to the chain link fence. There were cops in brown uniforms, blue ones, tan ones, and even black ones. They were pulling forces together for this annual event. This made Jess become even more frightened of her surroundings. "Are there cops on the inside of the fence?"

"No. There is no police protection for anyone who goes beyond those gates. And once you are in, you are not allowed back out until tomorrow morning."

"Are you sure you want to do this?"

"I've done it before. Besides it's too late to start back now." He couldn't tell her why he had to stay and why he was really there. "Don't worry as long as you're with me you will be safe."

"I hope you're right."

"Wow, that's a lot of faith."

She just shrugged and said nothing.

As they came closer and closer to the gates, Jess kept repeating in her mind what Toby said about no police protection beyond those gates. These must be the gates of hell, she couldn't seem to let that phrase escape her. She held her breath and said a prayer as they passed through the gate. Then, just beyond the gate Toby stopped.

"Jess, you see to the left there, at the carnival rides?"

"Yeah."

"And to the right, the camp grounds?" He was holding up traffic but he didn't care. He needed to explain what was fixing to happen next.

"Yeah?"

"You see those lines of guys?"

There were two lines. They all looked like a bunch of dirty bikers straight out of a *Hell's Angels* movie. Some had hair down to their rears. Some had hair braided, pony tailed, or not. Most all had on some kind of head band maybe an earring or two. Either no shirt at all or a jacket displaying their patches and colors they had so proudly earned in their gang. Jeans of all sorts and cut offs were also being worn.

"Yeah, I see 'em."

"That is the welcoming committee. Watch carefully how the two bikers in front of us go through."

They each had a girl on the back of their bike. The girls would pull off their tops, exposing their nakedness. They would then drive between the long lines of the welcoming committee.

The welcoming committee would do whatever they could to the woman's body in that brief moment. Whatever they did they had to do quickly because the biker would not stop but drove slowly. "Oh, my gosh! I can't believe it. I have never seen anything like it."

"Do you want to be welcomed?"

"No, I do not!" *How dare he think such a thing?* She then looked down and was reminded of why he could think such a thing.

"Then lock your arms around me and hold on tight." Chad waited until the last biker in front him had cleared the lines. He revved up his engine and took off.

Before he even reached the beginning of the line all the whooping and hollering began. "Chicken, *Bawk, Bawk,*

Bawk," and a few vulgar things were being screamed at them.

Jess held on as tight as she could and buried her face in between Chad's shoulder blades. As they sped through the lines, they were pawing at her blouse trying to rip it off. This couldn't really be happening to her. These were only things that are normally shown on TV. But this was not TV, and she was not in a movie. This was real. What would happen next? She couldn't even open her eyes not even when she no longer felt the anxious hands tearing at her. She hadn't even noticed that the bike had come to a stop.

"Are you okay?"

"Yeah," she said as she began to lift her face. This was another one of those times she was glad that Toby was not a dirty biker. He smelled fresh and clean even after riding all night in the wind. And he was wearing some type of musk oil that complimented his own personal scent very well.

"Are you sure you're okay?"

"Yeah, why?"

"Your knuckles are turning white." He looked down at her tightly held together hands that were wrapped around his chest. She had truly held on for dear life. He enjoyed her pressed up against his back like that.

"Oh, I'm sorry. I guess I forgot to let go."

Chad was not at all displeased in the way she released the tight grip on her own fingers as she let her hands fall gently to his sides.

CHAPTER EIGHTEEN

Jess began to notice the happenings around them as they slowly began to take off again. To their left a Rolling Stones photographer was snapping away at two women, standing nearby, letting two baby raccoons nurse from them. The facial expressions and body movement that these two women displayed before the cameras were disgusting. All around them there were acts of sexual pleasure being performed or put on display. Live nude models, both male and female.

"Are you okay?"

"*Noooo*," was her slow, long, drawn-out reply.

They soon came to an area of campers. Toby pulled off the path of the road and came within a few feet of a tent. Nearby were a couple of people standing around laughing and drinking beer. He stopped the bike before getting too close to the small crowd of drinkers. "Wait here, Jess, and whatever you do don't get off this bike. Okay?" She nodded in the affirmative.

"Don't worry, no one will come and snatch you off my bike. Not with me being so close to it."

"I'll be fine." She was reassuring herself.

He walked over to a couple of the guys standing near the tent. Jess could not understand what they were saying but she could hear the tone in their voices. She listened to see if she could detect any hostility or anger for what she assumed Toby was asking them to do. They never raised their voices at each other and they never took the smiles off of their faces. Was this good news or bad? Are they thinking of me as being stupid or are they plotting something for me that I want no part of? She had survived so far. And she would do whatever it took to survive again, if needed.

Jess thought for a minute that her mother must have been praying for her this morning. She hoped that the prayers that went up for her had not been all spent. She was now watching Toby stroll his way toward her. He really did look good. All muscle, no fat, beautiful white teeth on a smile that never seemed to leave his face. "I hope that smile means good news for me…and you."

"It does. The easy part is over. Now comes the hard part."

"What's the hard part?"

"I have to work out an agreement with Zack, the president of Skull & Cross."

"How will you do that?"

"We will ride over to where they are camped. And I will tell him that you belong to me. I know you really don't; so don't get mad at me. But we must make a believer out of him." And he wanted her to believe, too.

"Oh! Okay." She really didn't know what else to say. She felt like she was on a merry-go-round. One minute she was gathering her thoughts on what to do to keep safe and the next minute she felt like she was watching something out of a movie but feeling every emotion of the actress playing her part. Would tomorrow ever come for her? Through all this chaos, she somehow had to stay focused on the moment and right now her main concern was survival.

They rode over to where Mickey's van was parked. They rode past it and turned down a path to the right. Chad stopped the bike and roamed his eyes over the Skull & Cross members, not saying anything at first. They in return were glaring at him and Jess.

"Jess, what about your friend Lisa? Do you want help for her?"

"Yes, if she wants out. What do you think will happen?" She couldn't believe what she was saying but she was not a mean or bad person. She couldn't wish this on anyone, not even Lisa.

"I don't think they will fight. We had a rumble with them last year and we won. I am the sergeant of arms for our club. I don't think they want any more of me again. But if they do, my club will back me up. You see, we are more than a club, we are friends and I think that is where we get most of our strength from. I'll be right back.

"Whatever happens, don't get off my bike. I'm serious about this, don't get off this bike, okay?"

"Okay." He didn't need to worry she wouldn't leave his bike unless of course they killed him and were coming after her.

Chad walked with confidence and dignity toward the vans that were parked amongst the bikes and bikers. Lisa made her way over to where Jess was sitting.

"Hey Jess, I hope you're not sore at me."

Jess was, and yet she felt sorry for her too. She was so young and had to be mixed up in the head to be running with a bunch of bikers. "Lisa do you want out?"

"No thanks."

"You can come with me and Toby, if you want to."

"Naw. I know what I'm doing." And with that she left to go over to where all the yelling was taking place.

Zack was in a rage. This was the first time Jess had seen the smile leave Toby's face. Zack was yelling and flapping his arms up and down. He must have been on something; he sure was hyped. All of Zack's members had gathered around the two that were having a heated argument. What if they jumped him right there and now? How would Toby's friends know to come and help him? Why had he parked, putting Zack's gang between her and his friends? At least if she were on the other side she could run back for help if needed. She stared at the big bike of Toby's. Nah, she knew she would never be able to drive this big machine. Just then the yelling stopped and Toby began his proud stroll back over to where she was. The smile had returned.

"Whew!" She sighed in relief.

Chad laughed. "You'd think you were the one over there arguing with Zack."

"I felt like I was. I was trying to think of how I was going to help you if you needed it."

He gently placed his hand on her ever so smooth face. "I told you that no matter what happened, you were not to get off my bike. If you want to stay alive out here, you better do as I say."

Jess didn't know how to receive this or if even she wanted to. She was not used to being talked to in this manner of authority. "I thought about that and was even wondering how I would teach myself how to ride this bike if they killed you or something."

He removed his hand and mounted his bike. "They wouldn't have jumped me here and now. It's not the way to do things. We would have set up a time and place and agreed upon weapons."

"Sounds like something out of *West Side Story*."

"Gang fights haven't changed that much. Occasionally you get jumped when unprepared but most of the time it's done in a well prepared way. Only, we won't be dancing."

They rode back to where Chad's friends were camped. Everyone seemed to be enjoying themselves. There were no unusual sounds of fun. Now that Chad and Zack were through hollering at each other, for now anyway. Chad parked his Honda beside three Harleys. They dismounted. He took Jess by her elbow and led her over to meet the rest of his club members that not only rode together but fought together.

"Jess, this is Rex and Shelly, John and Marcie, Billy and Steve. Guys, this is Jess."

They all exchanged their hellos. "Jess would you like a beer?" Marcie asked, "Or a coke?"

"Yes, a coke would be fine. Thank you." She was looking each one over. Billy and Steve were two young guys about the ages of seventeen, eighteen, or nineteen. They looked like normal teenagers sitting around joking and laughing at silly things. The president, Rex, was a little overweight. He had long hair, a beard, and a rugged-aged face. But when he laughed or talked, he sounded real gentle. Jess guessed him to be nearing forty. Shelly, his wife was also a little overweight. She had long light brown hair that had plenty of natural waves. She had a soft friendly face. John and Marcie looked like any ordinary couple you wouldn't mind being seen with anywhere. She assumed they were married because they wore matching wedding bands. No, this gang of friends did not fit the description of filthy bikers, even though they all had on some kind of blue jean jacket, Tee-shirt, and blue jeans. They all had long hair and wore bandannas, leather and chains, but they were clean and friendly.

"Jess, Toby told us a little about how you got here." Shelly was telling her. "I think it's awful, some of the things gangs do. About recruiting, I mean."

"You mean you agree with the things they do to earn patches?"

"Oh no, we don't like those initiating things either. That's why our club stays so small. And we're really nobodies when it comes to who's who in the biker gangs."

"I'm glad of that. I mean, I'm glad for my sake." Jess did not want to offend Shelly or any of them that heard her comment. Shelly really did not seem to fit in with what Jess thought a female-bike lover would be like. But then again maybe even she didn't know what one was really like. After all she had been fooled by Lisa.

"Listen, you are welcome to be here with us anytime you want." Rex was saying.

"Thanks. And I don't mean to hurt anyone's feelings or anything and I sure am thankful for all your help. But I think if I ever get out of here alive, I'll probably not want to even see another bike for a while."

They all laughed. "You haven't hurt our feelings none." John said. "Just try and enjoy it while you're here. And try not to be so shaky. No one's going to hurt you here, as long as you keep Toby by your side."

"And the Skull & Cross have been warned already. I don't think that after last year's fight with them they'll try anything while we're around," said Rex.

"Yeah, we'll bust some heads like last year." Steve was saying and punching around on Billy.

"Hey! Watch it, man. I'll lay you out." Billy was pulling away and straightening his sleeveless jacket.

"You see, Toby here is our sergeant at arms, as long as you're with him they'll leave you alone."

Jess was watching Toby blush a little for the first time, yet he squared his shoulders back. She could see that he was proud of himself. "Just what does a sergeant at arms do?" she asked.

Rex placed his overweight hand on Chad's muscular upper arm. "He first fights the sergeant at arms of any other gang that wants a piece of our gang...or club. If Toby wins then we choose the fight and weapons. If he loses then they choose."

"And what kind of weapons do you use?" Jess was getting an uneasy feeling in her stomach.

"Fists mostly, but we keep our chains and knives close by, 'cause you can never trust these wild gangs to be fair," Rex told her.

"I thought you said you weren't a biker gang, Toby."

"We're not. Not like the one Lisa is with. We're really just a group of people that got together and like bikes. But we don't agree with the way biker 'gangs!' do things. So we have to fight in order to ride together and come to these conventions. So we are sort of a gang but not like others." Chad was trying to explain.

"You see Jess." Marcie was telling her. "That's why when Toby came here and told us what had happened to you, we all agreed that you needed help. We would do it for anyone, especially if that someone had been tricked into it."

"Yeah, we need to talk about that." Chad said.

"Yeah, we do." said Rex. "You know I was telling you that as long as you stayed close by Toby nothing would happen to you?"

"Yeah."

"If we don't make Zack think you belong to us now, then when we get back to Memphis they won't leave you alone," John commented.

"What are you saying, John?" Jess was getting worried at this statement. Were they going to try to initiate her the way Skull & Cross were going to try to do...or even worse?

Chad could see the fear in her eyes. "No. No, Jess, nothing like what you're thinking."

"How do you know what I'm thinking?"

"I've seen the looks on your face today with everything that's been happening to you. I can tell that you are afraid still."

"I don't mean to make you think I'm not grateful for what you have done. It's just that I have been lied to so much and tricked so horribly. I just don't know how to trust anyone anymore."

"That's fine sweetie, we all understand." Marcie came over to her and put her arm around her shoulder. "You guys are scaring her. Can't you see that?"

"No, No, I'm okay really. I'm fine now. So, go on, explain to me what you're talking about."

Chad started again. "Jess, we have to make them think you're my woman. That doesn't mean you are or that you have to do anything against your will, it just means that while we're here you mustn't be seen anywhere without me by your side. You shouldn't even go to the bathroom without me walking you there and even leaning on the door to prove that your mine."

"You see, Jess, things around here are much different than the way people normally live. Even the gangs when they're away from here live differently." John said.

"I can see that. Go ahead." Jess said.

"They don't really live that much differently away from here, at least publically. But they show more openly and freely their way of doing things, while they are here," Shelly clarified.

Toby continued. "Jess, it's like watching a caveman movie. You know, where the caveman sees a woman he wants, and if he catches her off guard or alone or even just a few feet away from her man, then he feels that he has the right to snatch her. Then either the guy she was with lets him have her or fights for her, sometimes to the death."

"You've got to be kidding."

"No, I'm afraid not. I'm not saying these things to try and scare you into staying close to me...Not that I would mind." Chad was smiling his best smile at her. Even to have her by his side the whole time they were to be here excited him. She was so beautiful. Chad knew that he would be the envy of many people this weekend when seen walking with Jess.

Chad continued, "But for your own safety, you really do need to listen to what we're saying here. Jess, you are a very beautiful girl and I'm sure that Zack's gang won't be the only ones watching for an opportunity to get their hands on you."

"Awe, thank you for the compliment, Toby, that's sweet. And I don't think you need to worry any. I'm sure I won't leave your side. Nor do I want you to leave mine. Please, tell me." She felt so awkward and vulnerable being in this kind of situation. She knew that she had no knowledge of how things happened here, or at any annual biker's convention. "Just what will happen when we get back to Memphis?"

Shelly spoke. "Jess, it is important that for at least two months you are seen with us, or most importantly with Toby."

"That's right, Jess." John agreed.

Two months. She could handle that. "Okay. So what? We date or something like that?"

"Something like that." Chad offered.

Marcie spoke up. "But a little more than that. Remember now, we have to make them believe that you truly do belong to Toby."

"Now, Rex and I live in a duplex on Sledge Street. Do you know where that is, honey?" asked Shelly.

"No, I'm afraid I don't."

Shelly continued. "That's okay you'll know soon enough. Well, anyway, Toby rents the duplex upstairs from us."

"You see, Toby and John both work at the Tirestone Plant. They both work the night shift." Jess could tell that Shelly was trying to break something to her gently. But the anticipation was beginning to be too much.

"Okay, so what are you trying to say?"

"Jess, you need to move in with us for a couple of months. Just until we think you're safe. You don't even need to use your own car. You need to be seen driving my car around, even back and forth to work." Chad was telling her.

"Jess, this is serious business." Rex said.

"This is too much." Jess was trying to take it all in. The whole time they had been talking, she was listening and noticing the events going on all around their little camping area. There were biker men literally chasing women around the park. She had yet to see a woman that looked like she didn't want to be chased. Fights were breaking out here and there. They all seemed to be playing games with their lives.

Jess just wanted to close her eyes and open them again to find that this was all a bad dream. But every time she closed her eyes and opened them her surroundings were still there. No, this was not just going to go away by her wishing it to.

"And what will happen to me if I don't come and stay at your place?"

Chad proceeded, "If they're not watching you… nothing. Do they know where you live?" She said nothing as she shook her head in the affirmative. "Well then, it would be my best guess that they won't just let this thing go unnoticed."

There was nothing else said for a couple of minutes. Then Jess found her tongue again. "Just give me some time to think this over. Okay?"

It was Marcie to the rescue. "Sure, hon." She came over and put her arm once again around Jess' shoulders.

"That's right, Sugar, you just try and put it all out of your head for right now. I think we have told you enough for you to chew on for a while. Guys, no more talking about this mess for a while. You hear?" demanded Shelly.

"Yeah, Shelly," they answered in unison.

Jess could tell that Shelly had a lot of pull, even over the president. "I think that's a good idea." Rex spoke.

"Yeah, me too. Say, Jess, how would you like to stretch your legs a bit?" Chad asked.

"That's a good idea. You two go walk around a bit." Marcie was saying as she helped Jess to her feet. "Go show her the carnival rides or the creek or something. But be sure to stay close."

"Yes, a walk would be nice. I think," Jess said unsure.

CHAPTER NINETEEN

"What shall it be first, the carnival or the creek?"
"Thanks, Toby. I think I'd like to go see the creek first."

"The creek it is then. Bye, we'll see ya'll later."

"Don't fall in. I hear the water's real cold." Steve said. Steve and Billy had nothing to say during all the explaining that was going on earlier. They knew that they were too young and too new at this to have an input. Steve was Marcie's nephew. And Billy was Steve's closest friend. Steve had a love for Harleys but cared nothing for the crazy ways of biker gangs. So he hung around his Aunt Marcie and Uncle John. Billy was not as crazy about bikes as Steve was, but he was Steve's best friend. It seemed that they were pretty much left to themselves to do whatever they wanted to.

The creek was beautiful. The water ran clear; you could see right down to the bottom.

"Look over there, Jess."

"Oh, my lord, I can't believe what I'm seeing," she laughed. Just a little ways down the stream were a couple of people washing their bike. They had their bike sitting in the creek while washing it, nothing unusual about that but to see this old man and old woman washing it in the nude.

"I've never seen so many wrinkles in all my life. Nor do I want too. They must be at least eighty."

Chad laughed with her. "Yeah, they do look pretty funny don't they?"

"It must be true love," She said as she turned to face the hill.

"Jess, it's good to hear you laugh for a change."

"I figure that if you had any plans to harm me, you would already have made your move."

"I would never do that."

"What? Harm me? Or make your move?" before he could answer her, "No. I'm just kidding. I think I know now. I really don't know how to thank you. I am and will be forever in your debt."

"I'll tell you what. Let's not even think about you owing a debt right now. And in a couple of months when it's all over then we'll discuss it. Fair enough?"

"For now." *Over, do I really want it to be over in a couple of months? This,* looking around at her surroundings, *yes, most definitely, but Toby? Ummm, maybe not.*

"Good, let's leave these two love birds and go see what's at the carnival."

"Good enough."

Chad gently placed his hand at her elbow to lead her up the hill in a northeasterly direction toward the carnival. There were all kinds of people. There were people dressed like the hippies of the sixties and seventies. The sixties hippies most all wore moccasins with belle bottomed jeans with no shirts on the men and straight tops on the women. Now the seventies styled male hippies wore either bell bottomed, hip hugger jeans and no shirts or a denim vest. The women either wore halters or midriff tops with their hip huggers. Then the biggest crowds wore boot cut jeans, no shirts or at least their sleeveless jackets that displayed their array of colors. The women wore all sorts of styles or no tops at all.

Just as Jess was taking this all in, Chad reached for her hand and held on to it tightly. "There's Zack's gang over there. I want it to look like we're together, okay."

"Okay, but do we have to walk that way?"

"Not too close. But just in case they decide to look our way. We want to make them think you're mine." Chad liked this idea. He was hoping that maybe someday she would choose for real to be his.

Jess looked over to where the Skull & Cross van was. She shuddered at the thought of what was going on in that van as she could see gang members coming out zipping up their pants. They were all so stoned they could barely walk or stand. She looked hard to see if she could get a glimpse of Lisa anywhere. She could not see her amongst the crowd. Jess stepped in a little closer to Chad's stride. He put his arm gently around her waist to assure her of his presence. She did not protest at this, especially as she could see some of the gang members watching her and making dirty gestures with their hands and bodies. They were screaming obscenities and yelling threats while saying her name. They were daring her to step away from Toby.

"Don't look at them, Jess. Just keep on walking by and pretending that you don't hear them."

"That's kind of hard to do when they know that I hear them."

"You don't want them to think you're afraid."

"Should I flip them off or something like that?"

"It's your choice. But before you do I must tell you that they'll take that as a challenge. I might be able to hold them off long enough for you to get away. But later on if I'm not around they'll get you."

"I think I'll not flip them off." She very much wanted to throw a brick at them instead.

"How did you meet Lisa?"

"It was out at McKellar Park. We just sorta started hanging around each other." She was silent for a few more steps. "I think we're in a safe zone right now. You can remove your arm, for now anyway."

He did, reluctantly.

"You know the more I think about it, it was Lisa who started the first conversation. It was about my car."

"It's a nice car."

"It's what's left of my marriage."

"Tell me about your marriage."

She talked while they walked, until they came upon something that should not be seen in public or anywhere. Only a few feet away next to a light-blue panel van, with a half-way made lean-to, was an orgy. Jess quickly veered her eyes directly in front of her feet. But she could not stop the sounds from coming to her ears. Her stomach was turning. She picked up her pace. She grabbed Chad's hand to hurry him through this disgusting place.

"Come on Toby. Let's get out of here."

"Sorry, Jess." Even Chad was embarrassed.

"Did we have to take this route, or why did we even have to leave the camp?"

"We could have stayed at the camp. I'm sorry. I just didn't think about all of the things that we might see. Try not to let it bother you. Just chalk it up to experience learned."

"Yeah, and I'll be sure to not learn it again."

"You really do hate this place. Don't you?"

"I really want to leave now and never come back."

"We'll leave first thing in the morning. I'd take you back to Memphis right now if I could. But..."

"Yeah, I know, once beyond the gate you can't leave until the next morning."

"That's right." He knew he was already going to be in hot water if something happened to Styles before they pulled out in the morning.

"Jess, I just realized something."

"What, Toby?"

"In order to get to the side of the park where the carnival is, we have to pass through by way of the welcoming committee."

There was a long pause as they walked on. Jess realized that she was still holding Toby's hand. She must be more scared than she thought.

"What will they try to do?"

"Nothing, to walkers, unless we invite them. I just wanted to spare you any more surprises. I don't think they will even notice us too much. Well, on second thought, I'm sure they'll notice you." He smiled greatly.

"Do you think it's safe? I mean right now I don't want to go back by that lean-to."

"Yeah, I'm sure that they're so busy welcoming the arrivals that they won't bother with us. Besides, we'll turn around if you change your mind when we get closer."

Jess didn't want to turn around at this time nor did she want to go any further. But she decided that she would hang on to Toby as if she were his and maybe they would get by the welcoming committee with no problems.

"I've got an idea, Jess."

"I'm open for suggestions."

"Great, because I may have thought of a way to make your visit here a little more easier."

"I'm listening."

"Let's play a game with it. Let's just pretend that we actually did come here together. Let's walk around in front of everyone as if we have known each other forever and that we do this all the time."

"What? Why?"

"If we do this and act like we are enjoying it then maybe others won't notice us as if we were walking around in fear."

"Toby, you're not walking around in fear. I am. Is it that noticeable?"

"Does a bear poop in the woods?"

"That bad, huh?"

"Yep."

"I guess I can try it. It's got to be better than walking around in fear all the time."

"Great. Shall I pretend you are my girl, I mean, just for show in front of everyone here?"

"I guess so. I mean if you think that is the safest thing to do."

Chad let go of her hand and put his arm back around her tiny waist. She still found it a little hard to feel comfortable after what she had been through so far. But she put her arm under his and around his waist. There was no fat. He was built solid. Muscle through and through and so good looking.

"I'll try to relax a little."

"I think that is the best thing to do. I mean I know that you didn't mean to be here. But you are, so don't let it ruin your whole weekend."

"Yeah, and besides, we're together after all."

He was so glad to hear her say these things. Not only was she beautiful, sexy, and a nice girl. But being with her until tomorrow would help him keep his mind off what he was about to do to Zack's gang. Chad's only hope was that Zack would still cooperate if his buyer needed to deal directly with Zack. And after what they had tried to do to Jess, he was more anxious to get these guys off the streets and locked up in some prison somewhere. He was almost as anxious to get back to Memphis as Jess was.

CHAPTER TWENTY

It was back at the first park where the tickets were sold that Chad and Styles had got together with the needed information. At that time of their conversation, Zack and he were hitting it off pretty good. Zack felt pretty good about meeting with Chad's buyer. It was going to be a good sell. And to get most of the stuff sold even before he was to meet with the boss of all bosses. He had made previous arrangements to meet with Rands on Sunday evening at seven o'clock on a dock off of Riverside Drive.

The Memphis police department and the DEA had watched another place out on South 72 Highway, at a warehouse behind a store named Blaze Paints and Pools. This place was believed to be owned by Vianneh and used as a front. They were never able to make any arrests. Once, they thought they had gotten lucky. Someone tipped them off that the shipment of goods were being moved on flatbed trucks. If the barrels were opened up, they'd find what they were looking for. Said it would be enough to hang Vianneh. It turned out to be a prank.

Maybe Denton Vianneh had made someone mad and they decided to try and scare him a little.

The cops didn't think it was all a loss. Before this, they didn't know that there may be connections with Vianneh and Blaze Paints and Pools. After that gain of information, they watched this place pretty close for a while.

Vianneh must have known who had this vendetta against him. Two days after the mistaken bust, Roy Smith, another night club owner and Vianneh's biggest rival, was found murdered. The case ended up in the unsolved murder files. The cops had their suspicions that Vianneh was involved, but were not able to prove it. They wanted Vianneh. And they wanted him bad.

———

Jess and Chad had made it past the welcoming committee with no problems. But were not able to escape the obscene things the welcoming committee had to offer for the late arrivals.

"At what time do they stop waiting for people to come in?" Jess asked.

"Pretty soon now, it won't be long."

They could hear the screams coming from the carnival rides. "Oh! Look a cotton candy machine. Let's get some."

Chad took her over to the cotton candy. "One cotton candy for the lady, please."

Jess was amazed to see so many adults with little children at this gathering.

"Here you are, sir," the attendant said. Chad paid the man and thanked him as he gave the candy to Jess.

"Thanks, Toby." She shared her cotton candy with him. They didn't ride anything but the merry-go-round. Jess didn't feel up to riding anything that might put her stomach in a twirl. She was trying to get it settled down.

They laughed and talked as they hung around the carnival area, well up into the darkness of the night. It was like not being where they truly were. The night was beautiful. Jess thought many times over how near to death she had come that day while keeping in mind the day was not over.

They made their way back to camp that night with much more enjoyment than earlier. Even though there were campfires to light their way, it was still dark enough to not be able to see too much of anything she didn't want to see. If only she could shutout the screams of pain she heard. They walked in silence as she listened. Screams of torture filled the air. The screams of rape were being carried by the wind all through the trees. But laughter was mixed in as well. It was sounds that Jess would probably remember for a very long time.

They approached their camp. More of their members had arrived and introductions were made all around. Every one there still seemed normal and some had even gone into their tents for the night. Chad took his pup tent off his bike and began setting it up. It was a two man pup tent. Jess knew nothing of setting up a tent. Chad enjoyed showing and teaching her the ways of the outdoors. She liked it just as well. They laughed at her mistakes and the time she tripped over a cord put in place by Chad, she fell right into his arms.

They sat around the campfire, roasted hotdogs and marshmallows and talked with each other for a little while. Then Jess decided she needed a bathroom break. She got up and began to look for one. "Jess, you need to go?" asked Chad.

"Yeah, I do."

"Come on. I'll take you."

"Go with me, maybe. But not take me." She still demanded her independence.

"Fine." As he took her elbow and lead the way, he totally ignored what she had said.

The porta-potty closest to them was only about sixty-yards away. He opened the door and checked inside. "Now don't be alarmed when you get ready to come out and you find me leaning against the door."

"You mean you really do have to do that?"

"You betcha."

She went inside and as quiet as possible, embarrassed the whole time, proceeded to use the toilet. When she tried to open the door, sure enough, she had to bump the door a couple of times to get him to move. She stepped out into the night's fresh air.

"Look over there." Chad pointed not more than thirty-yards northeast of the porta-potties.

"Yeah." She wondered what was so different. It was just another group of bikers doing their thing.

"Those are the Hell's Angels."

He said enough. She took hold of his arm and began to walk toward their camp, nearly pulling him with her. He knew she was really afraid and he didn't like the reason why. He wished she could trust him to protect her and enjoy their time together.

As they arrived back at the camp, Chad took a roll of blankets and put one in the tent and one outside the door of the tent. "You can sleep in there. I'll sleep right out here by the door."

She didn't know what to say. With everything else that had happened that day she had not even thought of the sleeping arrangements.

"Are you sure you'll be all right?"

This is not what he wanted to hear. What he wanted to hear was her inviting him to sleep inside with her. "I'll do fine right here. Trust me, Jess." And he opened the tent flap to let her in.

She hadn't been in the tent more than thirty minutes or so, feeling comfortable, when it began to rain. It wasn't a heavy rain but enough to make you want to come in out of it.

"Toby." Jess was staring at him almost eye to eye through the tent opening.

"Yeah, Jess."

She whispered, not wanting anyone to hear her. "Toby, please, come inside."

She didn't have to ask him twice. "Thanks, Jess," he said as he spread his blanket next to hers.

"It's raining and I couldn't very well let you sleep out there in it, when this is your tent to begin with. And you have been so kind to rescue me and let me sleep here."

"Listen, Jess, I haven't rescued you. Or at least don't put it like that. You make me sound like some kind of a hero. And I assure you I'm not, okay. So, if you would… please stop saying that?"

"Sure." She was taken back a bit by that.

They lay in silence for a few minutes and then they talked quietly into the night. Chad made sure he didn't fall asleep until after she did. He didn't want to leave her awake and afraid and him not be awake to comfort her if need be.

The screams of both excitement and pain, the sounds of laughter and cries and the noises of enjoyment and sadness all could be heard throughout the night. Jess finally fell to the rescue of peace and quiet found only in her sleep.

When she awoke very early in the morning Chad was leaning on one elbow while resting his head in his hand, staring at her. "Morning, beautiful" he said.

"Morning." He had been the perfect gentleman all night. He hadn't made any moves on her.

"You are truly a gentleman, Toby."

"Why, thank you, Jess. It wasn't easy, let me assure you." Chad was speaking truth from within. He found it so hard not to touch her, but he wanted their time together to be special and he wanted it to last. He couldn't wait to tell the truth about who he really was. He wanted to hear her say his name Chad. He longed for that day.

"Jess, we better get up and pack up the Honda. It's early and not many people are stirring yet. I want to spare you the trouble of experiencing any more discomforts."

"Okay, Toby. That's sweet of you." Maybe he wasn't so bad. But then there is this club and his hanging around bikers. No. It probably wouldn't work. She'd want no part of this after it was all over in about two months.

As they left the solitude of their little tent, Jess saw Rex and Shelly loading up. They had already prepared breakfast, ate their part and were getting ready to leave.

"Better grab a bite before the others get up," Rex said.

"Sure, Rex. Hey, listen, we'll be ready to leave in about ten minutes. Can you guys wait? We'll ride back with you," Chad suggested.

"Sure. No problem. That okay with you Shelly?"

"Yeah, sure. No problem."

"Listen, Jess, stay here for a minute with Shelly. I'll be right back; there's something I must do." He needed to make contact with Styles without anyone knowing what he was up to. He walked away and almost as quickly as he left he was back. It turned out that Styles was headed in his direction and they exchanged knowing glances. It was time to pull out.

"Jess, grab something to eat while I take down the tent and pack up." She moved over to where the food was and fixed herself a plate of scrambled eggs, a roll and a piece of bacon. As she drank some orange juice and ate her breakfast, she watched Chad quickly and skillfully take down and pack up his little tent. He was ready by the time she finished her breakfast. She carried him a cup of orange juice.

"Thanks, Jess. That's all I want, nothing to eat for me." He swallowed it down in one drink.

"Let's go use the restroom before we leave." She fell right in step behind him.

Chad stopped and moved over to her side. "Jess, I'll not have you walk behind me, I want you beside me." They then walked beside each other with him placing his hand gently in the small of her back to lead the way.

It was a quiet morning; the dew was fresh on the grass and tree leaves. The sun had not yet dispelled all the darkness around them.

But there was enough light to see the hordes of people laid out all over. Some were in campers or tents and some were not. Some were on blankets or a sleeping bag and some were just lying out on the bare ground.

"Jess, look over there." Chad pointed up a hill to the far right. Walking across the hill was Lisa. She almost had a skip in her walk. She even had a smile on her very bruised face. Jess just shook her head and had to fight back the tears. Many emotions were running through her at this sight. Those of pain and sorrow mixed with those of confusion, not understanding why anyone would want to do this and seem to enjoy it. Emotions of thankfulness, knowing that could be her. No, she still felt for sure that she would have died fighting, if that were possible. Or maybe, worse, she would have had to live in shame the rest of her life, had it truly not been for Toby.

As soon as they reached camp, more people were beginning to stir all around.

"Let's go," Chad said.

"We're ready." Rex climbed on in front of Shelly, already sitting on their bike.

"Jess, you ready?" Chad asked.

"Since yesterday."

By the time they reached the gates, the camp grounds had come alive. Jess could not believe the relief she felt as they passed through what she called the Gates of Hell.

"You know, Toby, I feel like I just came out of the Gates of Hell."

"Oh yeah? I guess for some it could be called that, but not for you. You escaped."

"Not totally. But the Gates of Hell did not prevail."

"What do you mean by that?"

"I'm not sure, but it's part of some words sung in a song at my mother's church. It's funny how I remembered that phrase just now. It actually says, 'The Gates of Hell shall not prevail', but I'm saying the Gates of Hell did not prevail."

"You go to church?"

"Well, don't be so surprised. I like church. I just don't go enough."

"I didn't know that."

"There's a lot you don't know."

"I'll have two months to learn. You are going to take our advice on staying with me... uh, us." He liked the sound of that, "Aren't you?"

"I'm still thinking on it." After all that had happened, she really wanted to discuss all this with her mother. She was beginning to see more and more about the wisdom her mother had.

"Do you like church?" she asked.

"I like church, I just don't go."

"Why not?"

"I don't know. Just haven't found one I want to go to, I guess. Maybe I'll go to yours with you sometime."

"It's not mine. It's my mother's, but I do go sometimes. Next time I go... Maybe you can go with me."

Chad just laughed and shook his head. It was just as he figured. No sooner than he would have her out of the lion's den she would become independent again. She was a typical stubborn woman.

CHAPTER TWENTY-ONE

The ride back to Memphis was much better than the ride up from there. Chad's bike was so comfortable, Jess had no idea one could ride so smooth and not allow you to get tired or feel unsafe. Of course, riding behind Toby was a lot different than riding behind Stoney and much nicer. Chad had given her one of his flannel shirts to wear over her shirt of yesterday. She was thankful. She didn't want her mother to see those awful markings. No, she would spare her mother that part of the story.

Just before reaching Memphis, it began to rain. So both bikes pulled under a viaduct to let the rain pass. Much to Jess' surprise, Styles pulled up right behind them. She clinched hold of Chad's arm.

"It's okay, Jess, he's just spying for them," said Chad. "You're going to have to trust me; we need to not say anything to him just now, okay. Don't worry; he won't hurt you here—not while he's away from them."

Rex and Shelly knew why he was there but could still sense the fear in Jess. They all waited in silence for about fifteen minutes before taking off again. Chad knew that they had to get to Jess' early so that he would have time to convince her to stay with him. He then needed to deposit her at his place, under the watchful eye of Shelly, before he would contact the Chief and tell him where the shipment would be and what time. It was going to be a long day for sure.

They finally arrived in the Big M town. When they came to I-55, Rex and Shelly went north as Chad and Jess went south, Styles followed behind them before exiting somewhere in Whitehaven before they entered into Mississippi.

It was only about ten minutes later when they pulled into Jess' parent's driveway. Jess was now going to have to face her parents about what had happened to her. She buttoned another top button of his flannel shirt. As they entered the house they found Jean, Harvey, Kara, and Bryant sitting in the living room watching TV. The room was silent except for the noise from the TV. Jess reintroduced Toby to her family.

"I know you left with Lisa. So, I'm anxious to hear the reason you didn't come back with her," said Jean. Harvey just sat there with a not so happy look on his face.

"Kara, if I could ask you and Bryant to leave the room for now, please. I would like to talk with Mother and Harvey alone."

Reluctantly, especially Kara, they left quietly.

Jess and Chad together began to explain everything that happened. He even told them about the night he called to find out that Jess had left already, and that had been when he made the decision to go. He hoped that later, if and when they found out the truth about him that they would understand and be forgiving towards him.

Jean and Harvey both were in shock of what had almost happened to their daughter. Jean held Jess in her arms. Harvey pumped Toby's hand and thanked him over and over again. Jean cried and praised Jesus at the same time for sending someone to protect Jess. Finally, when everyone had gathered themselves, Jean and Harvey both agreed without reservation that Jess should stay in Toby's apartment. Jean assured her that Topper would be okay with them for a while.

Kara listened to every word her sister and mother were rapidly speaking as they quickly packed a few things for Jess to take with her. They hugged and said their good-byes before Chad and Jess took off.

Jean was still thanking Chad and praising God for protecting her little girl as they drove away.

The shipment was to arrive at seven that same evening. It was nearing five when Chad and Jess pulled into his driveway. He helped her get settled in and took her downstairs to Shelly's and explained that he had some business to take care of. Jess felt uneasy being left there and tried to convince Toby to let her ride along but he knew he couldn't do that—no way, no how. He held her close as he said good-bye and assured her that she would be fine and that he would be back as soon as he could. He gently kissed her forehead. He raced to the precinct to find Kyle, Penny and the Chief waiting. Everyone exchanged their hellos.

"It's about time. You're running at least an hour and a half behind. Would you care to explain?"

"Later, sir. It's nothing really, but we still have time to get there and get set up before they make the drop."

"Where?" the Chief asked.

"Sir, we better go. I'll explain on the way."

Kyle couldn't wait to hear about his trip and everything that had happened. He could tell that something took place that Chad didn't want to talk about in front of the Chief, so he anxiously waited.

Chad drove them right to a loading dock at the Mississippi river just off of Riverside Drive. "We better park a couple of blocks from here and then walk in and set up in hiding."

"Yes, sir," Chad said.

"Styles should be here in about ten minutes, Chief."

There were plenty of officers waiting on the streets nearby. Penny and Kyle helped put the wires on Chad. They were tested. Just as they were finishing up, they noticed a headlight coming in their direction. Hoping it was Styles, Chad walked up the street alone to be in the pathway of the biker. It was Styles. Chad motioned him over and hopped on the back of his bike as they rode away from the direction of the Chief and the others. Styles drove down Beale Street to make it look like they were out cruising the sights. They made their way back up to Jefferson and turned back west. They soon were in the same alley as the Chief. This was the second encounter Styles had had with their chief. He didn't like him at all. The Chief didn't like him either.

They continued discussing what would happen to each response that they anticipated. Styles stated that Vianneh, the Mayor and Rands were expected to be present when Zack brought in the shipment. Chad knew that he and Styles would be side by side. Styles had been instructed to stay close to Chad. Styles and Chad mounted the Harley, and once again they cruised Beale Street, this time heading back towards the river. They drove north on Riverside Drive until they came to the loading docks. They were alone, or so their eyes told them, but their minds knew otherwise.

—◦◊◦—

Jess had enjoyed her meal of spaghetti with Rex and Shelly. She could see why they both were a little overweight; Shelly was an excellent cook. Jess and Shelly cleaned the kitchen together as they talked about their childhood and such. Once in a while Jess would bring up something about Toby to her. She would answer shortly and change the subject. Jess soon decided not to approach talking about Toby to her again.

Jess made her way outside and up the stairs to Toby's apartment. She had time to browse around and look at how he had made his place neat and homey-looking. He had pictures of his parents, she assumed, pictures of lots of nice looking people. He had a picture of one of his nieces at the age of one or two. His niece was now fourteen, but Jess didn't know this. She assumed that this was his daughter, Heidi. She just couldn't understand why this picture looked old. But everything here looked old. Jess snooped around in his bedroom and found his badge and ID, Chad Daniels. She kept searching till she found a few reports that had not yet been turned in. She read them all. She realized that this was not Toby Nelson; there never was a Toby Nelson. She was putting this puzzle together now. She was fuming about all this at first and angry, and then hurt that he had lied to her. It was going to take her awhile to forgive him, if she decided to at all.

Jess decided to go outside and sit on the front-porch swing downstairs. She needed to cool off. She sat there with a glass of iced tea thinking things over. She noticed that Sledge Street was a quiet street, dark but quiet. The interstate was close enough to be heard, and of course living in Memphis, sirens of some sort could always be heard in the distance. Jess heard the boards behind her squeak. She turned just as a dark cloth bag was pulled over her head. She never saw her attacker.

When she came to, she pulled the cloth bag off her head. She was lying on an old green vinyl couch in an office of some sort. Her head was pounding. She checked the huge metal door. It was locked. She pounded for a while but never heard anyone. There was no phone. But, there was a filing cabinet. She began searching for clues as to where she was. She found files that contained shipping documents pertaining to items of decorations such as Ming vases imported from China and then shipped to other foreign countries. The files contained information about how drugs were being smuggled in vases and such from a loading dock off of Riverside Drive. Jess had a lot of reading ahead of her. *Oh well, I might be here a while,* she thought as she settled herself on the couch with papers in hand.

CHAPTER TWENTY-TWO

"Hey, man, you nearly blew it yesterday with Zack because of that chick," Styles was saying.

"Shh. Be quiet, man." Chad knew the chief was listening in.

"I thought you had to be crazy, riding off with that chick like that; stealing her right out from under the gang. Man, you've got to be crazy."

The Chief and everyone else listening through the wires attached to Chad could hear this conversation. Chad visualized the angry look his Chief probably had right now after hearing this.

"Yeah, and, what did Zack say?"

"He was sure ticked-off for a while. But you know how it is after a fix or two, he nearly forgot all about it."

"Yeah, let's hope he don't remember or hold it against me when he sees me here tonight."

Back at the equipment van, the Chief grilled Chad's partner, "Now, what do you think he's talking about, Kyle?"

"I don't know, sir. Honest, I don't have a clue." Chief Green looked at Penny.

She just offered her hands to the air to suggest that she didn't have a clue either.

"Well, all I got to say is this bust better go down. If it gets screwed because of Daniels letting some chick get in the way, I'll bust him myself. He'll never find a job in this town."

"Here they come. Toby, you ready?"

"Yeah, let's do this." Chad hoped that the Chief could still hear him.

A black Cadillac pulled up and Rands got out. The silhouette of two men could be seen, one sitting in the passenger seat and one in the back seat. In the lighting, it wasn't clear if they were Vianneh and the Mayor or not, but Chad suspected it to be so. Chad tried to keep his back turned toward the Mayor, fearing that for some reason or another, the Mayor might connect him with the city police. The Mayor and Chad had never really met or spoke, but they had been to some of the same functions from time to time.

"Styles?" Rands asked.

"Yes, sir. Sir, this is Nelson, the other buyer's representative I was telling you about," Styles said.

"This is a bit unusual, asking to see how smooth things go down in a deal to see if you're interested in a future buy," said Rands.

"Yeah, it's also unusual to let someone in to see how smooth things work," replied, Chad.

"Styles and Zack both said you could be trusted."

"That's what they said about you and your partners. I told them I was very skeptical about dealing with a city official, thus this meeting. You know as well as me, there's a lot more money involved from my buyer than you've probably ever dealt with. If this works smoothly then we'll buy again and again." Chad was watching for his reactions to see if he was buying his story.

Everyone flinched at the sound of tires crunching on the pavement as Zack and a few of his men arrived. Zack carried a briefcase over to where they were standing. "Let's go inside," Zack said as he nodded with his head. It was just the day before he'd sworn to Chad that once this deal was over, they would settle. Chad could tell by the way Zack looked at him he hadn't forgotten that promise.

Zack and his bodyguard led the way, Rands and Chad fell in step next, Styles was told to wait outside. It was at this time that Vianneh got out of the Cadillac and brought with him a case with the money inside. They all entered through the metal door of the building. Zack still glared at Chad. He didn't like him, but he liked money and would do whatever it took to get it. It had not been Zack's idea to let anyone be there to watch their proceedings but this is what his boss requested. "You got the money?" he asked.

"You got the stuff?" asked Rands.

Simultaneously, they opened their perspective carriers. Pleased at what each saw, they exchanged carriers and began to exit the building.

"Green. Green. Can you hear me?"

"Yes sir, Mayor. I hear you. We're ready."

"They just went in. What's going on?" You could hear the urgency in the Mayor's voice.

Kyle and Penny quizzically stared at each other, and then at their Chief.

"I'll explain later...Mayor, they're making the swap now. Move in men. You hear me? Move in now."

The Mayor quickly got out of the backseat of the car, moved up to the driver's seat and locked the doors.

"I couldn't let anyone know about the Mayor, not anyone." The Chief was explaining. "I have to follow orders too, you know."

They were running out the door of the van as the Chief was telling them this. Boy, would Chad be relieved to know that our town was being run by a good mayor. They were all relieved.

The warehouse door flung open, and there was much commotion going on in the shipyard. Zack tried to shut the door, but only to find himself standing face to face with Chad. Chad held his gun in Zack's face. "You're under arrest, Owen."

Zack Owen was quick with his hands. He knocked Chad's gun out of his hands and ran to his bike. Bullets were flying. Chad was quick on his heels, but not quick enough. Owen was getting away. Chad found his gun, jumped on Styles' bike and took off in pursuit of Owen.

They raced down main street where vehicles were prohibited. The only people there were the drunken partiers, winos, and homeless trying to bed down for the night. Chad ducked bullets and returned the fire as they drove past store fronts and businesses. Occasionally they shot out glass windows or doors.

Zack's bodyguard, Rands, and Vianneh tried to make a run for it but were pursued on foot and were quickly surrounded, but not before many shots were fired. Rands was hit in the leg and Vianneh was nicked in the shoulder. They were rounded up, handcuffed, and put in squad cars that now filled the parking lot with sirens and blue lights.

The Mayor now got out of the car and came over to where the chief was standing. They listened together as Rands and Vianneh were read their rights. "Great job, Chief," said Mayor Braxton.

The chief nodded in affirmation. "I didn't work alone."

"Sure, you didn't. Of course not," Braxton said as he and the chief walked away together.

—◦◦◦—

The chase led on. Chad had to put in another clip before shooting again. They made their way into Riverside Park, Chad still on Zack's tail. He could hear sirens as officers in patrol cars tried to keep up. But a patrol car was no match for a bike in tight quarters.

Suddenly, Owen had to swerve to miss a drunk staggering out into the road. This caused Owen's bike to hit a curb and then a rail that sent him and his bike through the air. Owen's bike fell first, into the Mississippi River, and Owen right after it. The current was pulling him down the river. Chad nearly laid the bike on its side as he skidded to a stop. He jumped off and ran to the river. He didn't hesitate to plunge in after Owen, so much for the transmitting wire. He grabbed him and they went under. They came up fighting. They fought their way back to the rocky bank. During the scuffle, Chad fell. Owen picked up a small boulder and was just about to crush Chad's head with it—a shot was fired. Owen fell to the ground and dropped the boulder. Chad rolled just in time to escape. Kyle fired the shot.

"Get up Owen." Chad pulled Owen to his feet. Blood was seeping through Owen's fingers as he held the bullet-hit arm. Chad gave him a couple shoves toward an officer. "Read him his rights."

Chad sat on a big boulder as Kyle made his way to him. "Thanks, man." Chad was saying while catching his breath. "I owe you one, partner." Chad put his hand on Kyle's shoulder for support as he stood.

"Don't mention it, partner."

"What about Vianneh, Rands, and Braxton?"

"Vianneh and Rands are being carried in. They'll get their day in court. Braxton was in on the bust the whole time. The Seller, as it turns out, was FBI."

"What? Really? Whew! what a night. Listen, I gotta go. Tell the chief I'll give a full report in the morning."

Just then another officer came toward them. "Officer Daniels, that guy we just arrested keeps saying something about a girl named Jess. Said you'd be interested in hearing what he had to say."

Chad and Kyle rushed to the squad car. Chad yanked Zack out by his shirt and slammed his back up against the car. "What do you know about Jess? Where is she?" He called him a few dirty words.

Zack Owen was laughing and holding his bleeding arm at the same time. Chad grabbed his injured arm and began to squeeze and twist it. This brought Owen to his knees. Chad cocked his gun.

"No, Chad." Kyle was tugging at his arm.

"If he wants to keep his arm he better talk."

"Hey Man! You better do as he says." Kyle tried to step between Chad and Zack. "He'll do it. Man, he'll take your arm right off." Chad shoved Kyle out of the way with Zack's body.

Fear crept on Zack's face as he was now staring directly into Chad's crazed eyes. "Okay, okay, she's at Blaze Paints and Pools." Chad threw Zack to the ground as he ran for Styles' bike.

"There's incriminating evidence stored there, but not for long. It will be blown to smithereens and so will that tramp of a girlfriend of yours." Zack was screaming out and laughing at the same time. "You'll never make it there in time," he yelled before being forced into the back seat of a squad car.

Chad was squealing tires as he left.

To get to Blaze Paints and Pools from Riverside Park in the daytime could take at least thirty to forty minutes. Chad hoped that driving at this time of night, he would get there sooner.

Kyle knew that Chad didn't need to be stopped by any patrolmen, so he was racing behind Chad in a squad car running his lights and sirens. He got on his radio to inform any and all patrol cars in the area.

Jess knew she had found incriminating evidence on someone named Jack Rands, Denton Vianneh, and also on Zack Owen. Now, she knew who had given her that bump on her head and why she was taken. This was to get back at Chad. She didn't know where Chad was, but if he was a good cop he'd find her. She looked around for something to put the papers in. She picked up the cloth bag that had been used on her. She stuffed as many of the papers as she could in it. Jess kept going to the door from time to time to listen for voices or movement of some sort. She heard nothing. After she zipped up the bag she, began searching the ceiling and walls for a way out. She soon resorted to banging and hollering through the door, hoping to draw someone's attention out there. Surely someone was there. Where were her captors? More importantly, where were her rescuers?

Chad reached speeds up to a hundred-miles-per-hour at times on the interstate. Kyle was right behind him. They both pulled into the parking lot of Blaze Paints and Pools with only about a minute to spare. Chad yelled at Kyle, "Turn the car around and get ready to get out of there."

Kyle did and then went to go help Chad; they had to shoot the lock to open the door. Chad and Kyle knew with all the chemicals that were there, an explosion would be intensified. They could hear banging and Jess hollering from the back of the storeroom warehouse. They rushed to save her.

"Stand back Jess!" Chad yelled.

Jess was relieved to hear his voice. She went to the couch and reached under it to pull out the cloth bag with the papers. Just then she heard more shots and the door flew open. Kyle was motioning for them to hurry up; he had already started toward the front of the building by the time Chad reached for Jess. He grabbed her arm and was pulling her out the door as she was trying to tell him what she had found.

"Jess, not now, we've got to hurry. There may be a bomb in here." He was yelling as he was pulling her out.

"A bomb?" She wasn't wasting any time now going with him. She was leading the way, following a ways behind Kyle.

The first explosion blasted just a few yards behind them. The explosions that followed were even closer, right behind their heels. They made it outside and into the car. Just as the car screeched out of the parking lot, the effects of the chemicals and explosions together caused Blaze Paints and Pools to go up into a huge fire ball.

Kyle was watching out his rearview mirror as they passed the fire trucks and patrol cars. Chad and Jess were watching out the back window with the heat of the flames beating on their faces. Chad took her in his arms and held her close. His clothes were still a little damp from the river but the race across town had dried him off some. "Jess, I almost lost you."

Her heart was pounding as they held each other. "Oh, Chad."

"Jess, you know?"

"I found your badge. I figured it out."

"Jess, I wanted you to find out another way."

"When we get back to your place, you can explain it all to me. So, if you're Chad...then who are you?" she asked Kyle.

Before he could explain, Chad told her. "That's Kyle, my partner. I'll explain later. Right now I just want to hold you."

Jess snuggled in closer to Chad. She was so happy to be there with him holding her like this. It felt right, like this is exactly where she belonged. She settled her head on his shoulder.

"We may have lost some incriminating evidence back there, but you're all that matters to me." Chad planted a light kiss on top of her head.

"No. You didn't lose it," she sat up. "At least I don't think you did. It's all right here. I think I've got it all right here. That's what I was about to tell you back there. Look." She opened the bag and began to show him the papers under the glow of the dome light. There was enough evidence there to keep Jack Rands, Denton Vianneh, and Zack Owen locked up for a very, very long time.

Chad took her in his arms again, "Oh, Jess, you are amazing."

"Chad, oh, Chad."

Oh, how he loved hearing her say his name. He never wanted to let her go and didn't plan to.

ABOUT THE AUTHOR

Cindy Grantham Brown began first writing stories in about the third or fourth grade. She recalls:

I remember in elementary school around the third or fourth grade, you know, when we were all learning about how to use the index cards at the school library to find a good book to read and how to write book reports. Well, I hated to read. So, I would just read the summaries of the books and make up my own stories. I thought, "Hmmm, if I choose a book by an 'Author Unknown' then my teacher couldn't find that book to see if my story matched the author's." Funny, how a kid's mind works. It worked for me, I always made good grades on my book reports, until the tenth grade when the whole class had to read an autobiography on the same man and write a book report. I knew I couldn't do it and yes, I had to go to summer school and repeat that class in order to pass to the eleventh grade.

Cindy grew up in and around Memphis, Tennessee. She attended Southaven High School in Southaven, Mississippi. She currently resides in Arkansas with her wonderful husband. Together they have six children; five are married, blessing them with eight grandchildren. She and her husband are both active members in their church and serve Christ Jesus, as their Lord and Savior.